# The Last Summer of Us

## MAGGIE HARCOURT

USBORNE

This edition first published in the UK in 2019 by Usborne Publishing Ltd., Usborne House, 83-85 Saffron Hill, London EC1N 8RT, England. www.usborne.com

First published in 2015. Text © Maggie Harcourt 2015

The right of Maggie Harcourt to be identified as the author of this work has been asserted by her in accordance with the Copyright, Designs and Patents Act, 1988.

Author photograph © Lou Abercrombie

Road trip beach at sunset © gradyreese/Getty; Man in rear window © ShripnikOlga/ Shutterstock; Newborough beach Anglesey Bay at sunset © Paul Nash/Shutterstock

The name Usborne and the devices ♈ 🌐 are Trade Marks of Usborne Publishing Ltd.

This is a work of fiction. The characters, incidents, and dialogues are products of the author's imagination and are not to be construed as real. Any resemblance to actual events or persons, living or dead, is entirely coincidental.

A CIP catalogue record for this book is available from the British Library.

ISBN 9781474955447  03562/5  JFMA JJASOND/19

Printed in the UK.

# *one*

"Limpet?"

Steffan has always called me Limpet, ever since the first time we met. Why should the day of my mother's funeral be any different?

"How're you doing?" he asks.

"You're seriously going to ask me that? Today?"

"You'll feel better when it's over."

"Did you?"

He shrugs.

Everything's off, everything's uncomfortable. Even the way he's looking at me: like he's still him, and I'm still me, but there's glass in between us, like we're somehow distanced from each other; different. In his case, it's the outfit. I would barely recognize him if I passed him in the street dressed like that: black suit and tie, and looking as smart as I've ever seen him – right down to the polished shoes. I've never really seen him wearing actual *shoes* outside of school before. Trainers, yes. Those ridiculous hiking boots he wore with shorts for the entire summer a couple of years ago? Sadly, yes. They were unforgettable – and not in a good way. But actual black-shiny-leather-shoes-with-laces? I can only think of one other time. I want to be normal, to make a joke, to smooth down his dark hair – which is still sticking up in spikes like a hedgehog with a headache, however tidy the rest of him might be – but his dad's waiting for him with a hard look on his face and I guess I'm not supposed to make jokes today.

Today I have to be…someone else.

It's been twelve days since my mother died; twelve days since the noises in the night. The sound of footsteps and the front doorbell seeping into my dreams. Twelve days since the voice in the small, dark hours of the morning, saying: "I think your mother's dead."

Steffan's barely gone inside before someone else says my name, and Jared's standing behind me. More at ease in his funeral get-up than Steffan – or me, because however hard I try to ignore them, my shoes *really* hurt – he looks like one of those Hollywood stars you see in old films. He does that. Look good, I mean. He has that Steve McQueen, young Paul Newman thing going on. Tall and blond and cool and broad-shouldered, with his hair swept back, looking like he doesn't even have to try. He probably doesn't.

Take today, for example. Jared looks like he's about to walk the red carpet. It's effortless for him. Meanwhile, Steffan looks like a backing singer for a wedding band. And me…?

Well, I look like crap. Moving on.

Jared, Steffan and me.

I guess the usual thing would be to say we're some kind of triangle, or a tripod, or something else that makes you think of the number three. Inseparable. Something which goes wibbly at the corners and collapses if all its sides aren't there. But us, not so much.

We're more like that poster you see on the wall in mechanics' workshops; you know the one? A triangle with the words *QUICK, GOOD, CHEAP* written along the sides (feel free to insert your own joke here, by the way – you know you were thinking it). The point is, the diagram's telling you that getting the combination to work is rarer than hens' teeth. The three sides of the triangle, however you look at it, always break down into "two-plus-one". You'll get a repair done quickly and it'll be good…but it won't be cheap. Or you could get a cheap, quick repair which won't be good…and so on. Same with us – in any number of ways, we're always two-and-one. Never quite three. But somehow, we kind of fit. You might not think it, but we do – that's why I like it; like us. We're…unexpected.

Jared, Steffan and me. Less the Three Musketeers, more the Mechanic's Paradox. Glamorous, right?

And by the way, if we *were* the Three Musketeers, I'd totally be Athos. Except for the shoes. I bet you anything Athos never had to put up with shoes like these.

Like everything else I'm wearing, they're new. New shoes, new dress, new bag. Normally, I'd be feeling pretty good about that – but the magic of it's lost on me right now. In the shop, I handed over the cash as the assistant folded the dress into tissue paper, tucking everything into a thick paper bag with woven ribbon handles. She passed it across the counter to me and smiled and said, "Treating yourself to a new outfit? Lovely." She meant it, too. I guess maybe to her it didn't seem weird for a sixteen year old to be buying a bunch of black stuff that makes her look like she's thirty-five or something. Maybe it's not – not in that kind of shop, anyway.

As if the shoes weren't enough of a pain, there's the thing with the flowers. Which is…awkward. The florists have forgotten to attach the cards to the wreaths, and apparently as I'm the one who organized them all, it's up to me to fix this. Me, and the funeral director – who I find kneeling by a pillar in the church, poking at the flowers and getting his black morning suit all dusty. A few paces behind him, a little knot of family are talking quietly.

The funeral director sees me coming and stands up, brushing his knees.

"I wondered whether you might be able to…" He nods

at the flowers. "I wouldn't want to get it wrong." Why he couldn't ask my dad, I don't know – and then, with a sinking feeling, I realize that he probably did. Like he'd be any use.

"Men and flowers, right? Clueless."

He blinks at me, and – exactly three seconds too late – I remember the *Be Somebody Else Today* rule. Keep your chin up and your mouth shut. Suck it up and choke it down. All that. So I try to look solemn and start matching cards to flowers as everyone takes their seats in the narrow pews, and I'm barely done before the coffin's at the door.

"Do you want to see her? Do you?" Twice, my dad asked me that, and each time I answered it got harder to stop my voice from cracking.

"No. I don't want to." Three thirty in the morning, and we were waiting for the coroner's officer. I made tea. It's what you do, isn't it? Don't ask me why, but when everything goes wrong, you make tea. So that's what I did. Constantly. The two police officers who'd come with the ambulance waited with us. At first I thought they were just being, you know…nice. But then a little voice in the back of my head piped up and asked whether it wasn't more likely that they were, essentially, guarding the body. Guarding my mother – or at least, what used to be her. The shell of her.

I ignored the little voice and made them tea. Lots of tea.

And to their credit, they drank every single cup.

Or poured it on the houseplants when I wasn't looking…

"Lovely service."

"Beautiful service."

"Your eulogy was perfect. You had her exactly right."

"Just what she would have wanted."

"Such a beautiful funeral."

The handshakes and platitudes go on for ever, and I feel like my skin is inside out: every part of me is just one big exposed nerve. I smile and nod and dig my fingernails into my left palm and remind myself that I'm someone else today and she will be keeping her cakehole firmly shut. Because no funeral is lovely. No funeral is beautiful – mostly because it's a fucking funeral and you only have them when somebody's dead. And my mother would, I'm sure, really rather not be dead. What she'd *want* right now is to be on a cruise around the Caribbean. Or lying on a sunbed by a pool with a stack of books. Not shut in a box that's about to be dropped down a big hole.

But today's not the day for telling the truth. Today's a day for lying, and pretending you don't know that everyone else is lying too. I'm not sure who I hate more: all of them for lying to me – lying *with* me – or me for almost believing them because it's what I thought I needed.

\* \* \*

It's done. Over. Dead and buried, and people are starting to move away from the graveside and towards the cars. Some are looking at the flowers. A great-aunt I think I've met twice in my life is crouching next to one of the wreaths, switching the cards round.

"Are you kidding me?" I say it a little louder than I probably should, but *seriously*? She stops and makes a loud tutting noise before scuttling off, clutching her handbag. She passes Steffan on her way to the cars, giving him a dirty look. He sticks his tongue out at her. Seventeen years old, and he still sticks his tongue out at people. He winks at me across the graveyard and I wonder whether it was more for my benefit than his.

Most of the funeral party have drifted off – after all, there's tea to be drunk and sandwiches to be eaten and the carcass of a life to be picked over. My dad's hanging back by the grave and I know I should go to him – but I just…can't. The hole's too deep and too cold and so very, very lonely. So I wait, leaning against a tree midway between grave and gate, getting hotter and hotter in this ridiculous dress in the summer sun, and when Jared slips out from behind the tree he scares the life out of me and I barely hold back a scream. I had no idea he was there; I hadn't expected him to wait. He gives me one of his Hollywood smiles.

"You going to move over?"

"It's a tree, Jar. It's, y'know…round?" I edge sideways, keeping my back against the tree. Making a full circuit of it, I slide all the way round and back to the front so I'm next to him again, on the other side to where I started. He doesn't seem impressed.

"Jokes? Today?"

"Piss off." I was doing so well.

We stand there, neither of us speaking for a while. And then he says: "Dad's back."

"That was quick. I thought he had another year before he got out?"

"Good behaviour, wasn't it?" Jared sticks his hands in his pockets. "Bet you a tenner he gave them the speech."

"He's got a speech?"

"Probably. He's had enough practice by now, hasn't he?"

"Are you okay?"

"Don't have much choice, do I?"

"What does your mum think?"

You'd have to be standing as close to him as I am to notice the way his jaw sets and his shoulders tighten before he answers. "Mum's moving in with Marcus."


Marcus is Jared's mum's boyfriend – the latest in a long line. The first time they met, Marcus took the time to sit Jared down and tell him, man to man, that he had absolutely no interest in building a relationship with him; that his mother was the only part of this package he was interested in. That he already had enough kids of his own and wasn't interested in raising someone else's, let alone some *scumbag convict's boy*, thank you very much.

We don't like him a whole lot. Jared's Jared, so he'll tell you it isn't a big deal...but wow. I mean, *wow*.

So Jared's father is back from his latest stay at Her Majesty's pleasure just in time to see his estranged wife move in with the latest loser, and as usual Jared's stuck in the middle and watching the whole show from his grandparents' place, which is where he spends most of his time these days.

And I thought I had problems.


The car ride is uncomfortable. Prickly. Silent. My father stares out of one window, I stare out of another. Never on the same side: why break the habit?

I never realized how big the space my mother filled was. You could put your arms around it and your hands wouldn't meet on the other side. And without her, without something solid in that space, my father and I are absolute strangers. Strangers with the same last name, and the same nose, sitting beside each other in the same car and mourning the loss of the same soul… But strangers.

A five-minute car journey has never, in the history of mankind, taken so long.

I picked the pub for the wake. It has roses round the door, rusty-red against the white paint, like blood on sheets.

I can't go in.

I was never going to.

Instead, I walk out of the car park, and turn right into the road. It's quiet – it always is round here – and even though I can hear traffic on the bypass, there's not a car to be seen. So I walk in the road, and I walk, and suddenly, without quite knowing when it happened, I'm running. Running in the stupid black shoes and the stupid black dress, away from the stupid pub and the stupid wake and the stupid, stupid people, right down the middle of the road.

I'm running to the bridge. To the river.

Thanks to the hot summer, the river's low and the ground on the other side of the wooden stile is dry, cracked and dusty soil instead of ankle-deep mud like it is in winter. There are potholes in the path where there are normally puddles, and pebbles big enough to turn your ankle over if you're not watching where you put your feet; forks branch off into the trees on either side, with the river close enough for you to land in if you don't know where you're going. But I do. I've spent my whole life here – here, or wishing I was here – and when I come to the tree with the twisted branch and the old nail sticking out of it, I know I'm almost safe and I step off the path and into the undergrowth.

It's cool in the trees, out of the sun. The shadows have kept the moss damp, and it's green and soft. There are ferns everywhere, and the heels of my shoes keep catching in tangles of ivy – so I take them off, and just hope no one's been chucking bottles about again. I trod on a roll of barbed wire here once when I was a kid. It's not an experience I'm keen to repeat, I'll be honest. But treading on the moss is like treading on pillows, and it tickles. Something pulls on the hem of my dress and I don't care. I don't care if it gets torn to shreds. Instead, I pick up my shoes and push through the branches, sliding down a steep grassy bank that smells like summer should...and there they are.

Steffan and Jared, waiting at the river's edge. With beer.

They've taken off their ties and their jackets and hung them on a tree. Jared's shirt is hanging open and he's sitting on a rock in the sun with his head tipped back and his eyes shut. Steffan (less movie star and a bit more...movie-set builder – and as self-conscious about it as ever) has his sleeves rolled up and is standing right by the water, poking at the bottles they've stashed in there to cool. It feels like there's half a conversation hanging in the air – bitten off and swallowed the second I appeared. I have enough grossed-out experience to realize that I probably don't want to know what they were talking about. Steffan takes one look at me and laughs.

"Come through the hedge backwards, did you?"

I'm not rising to it. Nope. Not me. But that's not because it's today, and it's not because I need to be someone else any longer. It's because I'm safe and I'm home and they were waiting for me.

And there's just one thing I have to do right now.

I pick my way down to the water...and standing right on the edge alongside Steffan, I throw my shoes as far into the river as I can.

Jared opens his eyes when he hears the splash and sits up. Steffan's mouth drops open.

I give them both my best smile and grab Steffan's open bottle of beer out of his hand, take the biggest swig I can manage, and throw myself down onto the bank.

"You're welcome," says Steffan, pointedly. He's not that bothered. There's more beer in the river. Besides, he's had plenty of time before now to get used to me, and today isn't the day he's going to have a strop. People who don't know any better usually think we're brother and sister when they see us together. Might as well be, I suppose – although I'm pretty sure my chin is nowhere near the size of his.

Neither of them tries to talk to me. Neither of them asks me how I'm feeling; if I'm alright, if there's anything they can do. Thank god for that. One more apology, one more lie, one more well-meaning sympathetic face and I'm going to smack someone. But Jared and Steffan, they wouldn't. Not here, not now. They know what I need more than anything.

Beer and the river and my friends.

Maybe not in that order.

So we're silent, and Steffan gets himself another beer from the collection they've wedged in the water with a pile of stones and opens it, and the current hurries on past us like we don't matter and that's just how it should be.

When we've been there long enough for the sun to have moved all the way round, and for there to be more empty bottles in the plastic bag beside Jared's rock than there are in the water, Steffan looks up from the label he's peeling off his bottle and says: "You know what we should do? Road trip."

Jared raises an eyebrow.

And I've had just about enough beer to say yes.

# two

Beeping. There's a beeping sound. Somewhere.

Somewhere in my room.

It's annoying.

Beep-beep-beep-beep-bloody-beep.

Being the genius that I am, I have forgotten to switch off my alarm clock and it's now jingling merrily away at me from the other side of the room, telling me it's funeral o'clock. Which it's not.

I'm still going to have to get out of bed, just to shut it up. I resent this. A lot.

Seven thirty in the morning is an ungodly time to be out of bed in the summer holidays. Until yesterday, I wasn't entirely sure there *was* a seven thirty in the morning in the summer holidays; I just sort of assumed the clocks skipped from somewhere around one a.m. through to nine o'clock or so. To punish my alarm clock for spoiling this illusion,

I stick it in my cupboard. That'll teach it.

Seven thirty. The only way I can possibly cope with this is coffee.

In the kitchen, I find my Aunt Amy. Or most of her, at least: she's perched on the window sill and has somehow managed to contort most of her upper body out through the open window. When I walk in, she twitches violently enough to almost fall out completely – but she catches her balance and comes back inside...along with a plume of cigarette smoke.

"Subtle," I say, filling the kettle.

"Don't." She shakes her head, looking embarrassed. There are dark circles under her eyes and she looks like she's aged five years overnight. Well. Maybe not overnight. Maybe over two weeks.

"You could just go out in the garden, you know."

"It's too early to be sensible. Are you putting the kettle on?"

I like my aunt. She's stupidly disorganized and is always late for everything, which makes her a lot like me. I haven't seen her smoke since I was little – she gave up years ago – but she just lost her big sister, so I guess it's not exactly shocking. Even so...

There's a pile of bin bags in the corner of the kitchen which definitely wasn't there when I went to bed. I shoot a look at Amy – who's taken the mug I passed her and is apparently trying to inhale her coffee – and she shoots one back.

"What's that?" I ask, pointing to the pile.

There's a second's pause. The look that crosses her face is complicated and I don't really understand it.

"I thought it might be an idea to…get rid of some old things." She sets the mug down on the table, and her hands are shaking.

"Mum's things?" I nudge the bottom bag with my toe. There's something heavy and solid inside it; *lots* of heavy, solid things, and they clank as they shift in the bag. I recognize the sound. Bottles. Lots of bottles. Bottles from where? Everywhere. Bottles from under the sink, from under the stairs. From the airing cupboard or the garden shed.

She pretends she didn't hear the sound. "No, not that. That's not what I meant. It's too soon, and I wouldn't do that without you. Or your dad." She adds him like he's an afterthought, which I guess he is, still asleep in the living room with the door closed. His world has shrunk to just that one room. He won't sleep in their…his…bedroom. It took him a week to even set foot in there afterwards. I changed the bed, picking up all the sheets off the mattress and the floor where they'd fallen and throwing them straight into the outside bin. What else was I supposed to do?

"Listen…" She pulls a chair out from the table and sits

down, rubbing the bridge of her nose. "I'm going to ask you something, and I don't want you to take it the wrong way. So can you, I don't know, try not to be a teenager for a minute?"

"Charming!"

"You know what I mean."

"What is it?"

"I think you might want to…not be here for a few days. Can you go stay with a friend, maybe?"

"Can't I stay with you?"

"I'm going to be here."

"Oh."

I should have picked up on it when I saw the cigarette. I sit down at the table with her. "You're going to be here? And you're asking me not to be? What's going on?"

"Look, your dad… He needs something. Some help. You know that, don't you?" She pauses, obviously not sure whether she should wait for me to answer. She decides to hedge her bets.

"He can't cope and I'm worried that—" I cut across her. "You know what? I can't hear this right now. I'm sorry. I just…can't."

A look of pain crosses her face and I regret it. I regret everything she's having to deal with and I regret the words that just came out of my mouth, the ones that sound like I don't care. I do care. That's the thing. I couldn't care *more*, not less. She bites her lip and her face smoothes itself out, the lines and the creases disappearing behind a mask. "There's someone coming to see him later. A doctor."

"And?"

"And I don't know what happens after that. A lot of it will depend on your dad, I suppose. How he wants to take things forward, what he wants to do."

"Oh." I stare into the bottom of my mug. The last few drops of coffee have started to dry into rings. Can you read coffee rings like tea leaves? I wonder. Will they tell me the future if I look hard enough? Will I like it?

Amy's watching me, waiting. She's treating me like a bomb carved out of crystal: one jolt and it's over for everyone in a twenty-mile radius. Maybe twenty-five. Her eyes are red. She's been crying, and I should say something – anything – but I've had almost two weeks of everybody else's feelings, and I don't think I can handle any more. So I don't. And when she asks me again whether there's anyone I can stay with, I say: "There's Steffan…"

There's always Steffan. Solid. Dependable. My Steffan. Ever since I fell down the steps on my first day of secondary school, and found myself being picked up again and set back on my feet by a boy with hair that stuck out in fifteen different directions and a school tie that had been cut off so short he could barely even tie it. He was an impossibly confident Year Eight compared to me, lost and bruised and embarrassed on my first day and scrambling to pick everything up and shove it back into my bag. And that was it. He was always around after that; like I say, I was the kid sister he never had.

It was me he called when his mum's cancer came back two years ago. I spent the whole of that Christmas in the family room at the hospital with him, while, across the hall, drips pumped poison into her in the hope of saving her life. They hit it hard, but it hit back harder and by the next Easter she was gone, and it's still the only time I've ever seen Steffan cry.

I remember sitting in the chapel, looking down from the gallery as he followed his mother's coffin in his own pair of brand-new shoes – the ones I've only seen him wear to funerals now – and I understood that one day it would be me in his place.

I never thought I'd be doing it so soon after him.

Is it better to lose someone slowly, or fast? Is it better to see them fade – knowing you're helpless to hold on to them and watching them slide into the darkness – or is it easier to have them torn away from you in the night? Easier to say goodbye a hundred times, never knowing for sure which will be the last, or to say goodnight and never speak again? Which hurts the least? I don't think either of us could tell you.

That first morning, when the coroner's officer and the police and the body had gone, when I'd thrown the sheets in the dustbin, when my father was locked in the bathroom with his mobile and a bottle of Scotch, calling what seemed like everyone he'd ever met to tell them his wife had died, and when my aunt was in her car, driving as fast as she could towards us… That first morning I knocked on Steffan's door and he opened it and took one look at me, and just like that he knew, and he put his arms around me and held me tight. He didn't know *all* of it then – there are some things you just can't say out loud at times like that, not even to your best friend – but he knew enough. He always does.

There's always Steffan. There always has been, always will be.

There's always Steffan, and up until this moment, I never realized just how much that means.

Amy nods and rubs her eyes, and I guess the conversation's closed. She looks tired. So tired. But I can't take on any more – not right now. So I push away from the table and slouch back up to my room and wonder whether I've actually got any clothes that count as clean enough to be worth putting into a bag.

From downstairs, I can hear snatches of my aunt's voice: she's on the phone, and although I'm trying not to listen – because, dear *god*, I don't want to hear – I make out the words "doctor"…"treatment"…"Steffan".

I switch the radio on, and start picking T-shirts up from the floor.

* * *

Amy's too distracted to be worried about my plans for the next few days. I'm a big girl, right? I'm suitably vague – and so is she.

I find my phone and send a hopeful text to Steffan: hopeful because it *might* occur to him to come and pick me up, him being the one with the car, rather than leaving me to walk all the way across town with a bag full of clothes. I know town's not exactly big, but that's not the point, is it? I carry on slinging things into my bag (toothbrush, deodorant, flip-flops, shorts, a jumper that probably needs a wash but which is just going to have to do) until my phone beeps. His reply is typically Steffanesque.

*You've been watching too many sappy films. It's two, three nights, tops. How much stuff do you need?!*

Right, so no chance of a lift, then. My second text is maybe a *touch* on the passive-aggressive side.

*What time shall I bring all my stuff over to yours, then?*

He pings back:

*Whenever. We're set. Just waiting for you.*

The sound of something being dropped in the kitchen – and Amy swearing – makes me jump. I'd almost forgotten that she was here. Almost forgotten...but not quite. I shove the last of my clothes into my bag – which is probably twice as full as it needs to be – and make my

25

way downstairs. Amy's listening intently to someone on the other end of the phone line. She holds up a hand asking me to wait, but I just want to be out. I want to go, to get away from here, this house and everything it means. Tapping my watch, I make the international sign for "I've got to go," and she nods. She smiles and points at me, then at her phone, and mouths the words "Call me." I nod back. As I pass the closed living room door, I think about knocking. But I don't.

When I walk out of the door, I can't stop myself from looking back over my shoulder. I don't know what I'm expecting, exactly: maybe to see a big black cloud hovering over my house? Whatever. It's not coming with me. I take a deep breath and set off down the street.

The sun's not as hot as yesterday – not yet, anyway – and there are birds singing, and the river's rushing under the bridge and there are cars on the bypass and everything feels obscenely *normal*. I guess this *is* normal now, though. The new normal. Everything that's happened in the last two weeks has been a kind of limbo: shifting from one normal to another. Now the funeral's done, it's all over and it's time to move on.

Steffan's car is parked in the driveway in front of his house, the bonnet open and a pile of bags on the ground next to the boot. There's no sign of either Steffan or Jared (who, living a hell of a lot closer than I do, must be here already – I'd recognize the tatty red rucksack with graffiti all over it anywhere) but the front door is open, so I dump my bag with the others and head inside to find them, following the sound of a radio.

They're in the kitchen and between them on the table is the biggest plate of bacon I've ever seen. I'm not kidding: this is Mount Bacon. Explorers could lose themselves on its lower slopes for a month; it must have taken at least fifteen pigs to make this much meat. And Steffan and Jared are cheerfully ploughing their way through it. It's either impressive or disgusting – I'm not sure which. Could go either way. It's not exactly a shock, though – I mean these two can *eat*. Jared's been banned from the school canteen for repeatedly finishing not only his own lunch but everyone else's too. In his defence, he did ask first – it's not like he swiped a handful of fish fingers from some starving Year Nine's plate – but apparently it's "inappropriate" from a senior. (If you ask me, I think the flirting with the canteen staff to get a third helping of cake every Friday lunchtime was probably the last straw.) As for Steffan, I've seen him put away an eight-egg omelette and still be hungry.

Sticking your arm into the middle of all that is a bit like sticking it into a bowl of cartoon piranhas: you kind of expect it to come back gnawed to the bone. However, I am brave. And I like bacon. I emerge triumphant, clutching two whole rashers and having my hand slapped at only once by Steffan. Feeling mightily pleased with myself, I perch on the closest worktop.

"Sure you want to eat that? You know it had a face once, right?" Steffan sniggers at me.

He's referring to my infamous vegetarian period, which happened when I was thirteen and lasted precisely a week and a half (and ended when I realized that almost everything I like to eat had, at some point, eyes, ears and a tail). You'd think by now he'd be bored of bringing it up. You massively underestimate Steffan's love of taking the piss.

I pull a face and they chew and the local radio DJ waffles on about the temporary traffic lights on the bypass and, dear god, does he not have anything better to talk about? This is the thing about living in a small town: however small it is, it might as well be the whole world. As far as some of the people who live here are concerned, the universe stops just past the end of the dual carriageway – and it only goes *that* far because the garden centre's off the roundabout, and if you lose that, you lose your begonias and your coffee shop with Sunday carvery. Mrs Davies who lives at number 32 in our road? She's never left town. Not at all. Not even for a holiday. Can you imagine? She's so comfortable here that she doesn't want to be anywhere else, to go anywhere else. She's content to simply be where she is; where she's always been. What a thought.

The bacon is gone. I know this without even looking at

the plate, because Jared's pushing his chair away from the table and no way does Jared leave a table with food still on it. I don't know where he puts it all: "hollow legs", my grandmother used to say. If that's true, then Jared's hollow all the way down to his toenails.

"What's the plan?" he asks, looking from Steffan to me and back again.

"Don't ask me," I splutter back at him. They've worked their way through the whole pile of bacon, and I'm still chewing my second piece. "This is his party." I wave my hand in Steffan's general direction. He responds by stealing the last bite of bacon from between my fingers and eating it, winking at me.

"No plan, is there?" he says. "Just us, in the car. Driving."

"Driving where, though?" I slip down from the worktop and wipe the bacon grease off my fingers with the kitchen towel. "You can't just...*drive*."

"Why not? That's the whole point of a road trip, isn't it? It's all about..." His eyes glaze over as he stares into the distance... "The journey."

"During which you usually see stuff. Or *do* stuff. World's biggest ball of string, Grand Canyon, that kind of thing? Hence it being 'A Journey' and not just 'three of us sitting in a car, listening to your dodgy taste in music'."

"I resent that. I have excellent taste in music."

"Yeah, right. Keep telling yourself that."

"Oi! I— Woah there. No." Steffan breaks off from insulting me and darts across the kitchen, slamming the fridge door shut. While he was busy Not Having A Plan, Jared's started poking around the cupboards. Honestly, he'd eat the furniture given half a chance. "Not the fridge," says Steffan firmly.

"Get in trouble for the beer, did we?" Jared doesn't sound even the least bit sympathetic.

"Not exactly." Steffan looks sheepish for a second. "Might do for this, though." He grins and jerks his head towards a flat, oblong box sitting on a shelf near the door. It looks like it's made of cardboard, and I haven't the faintest idea what's in it. There are what look like flowers and women in flouncy dresses printed on it, and some kind of gold sticker sealing it shut. The seal's been broken.

"What's that?" I ask, but neither of them pays me any attention. Of course they wouldn't: it's two-plus-one. Two in the know, one not, in this case. Mechanic's Paradox, remember? Always the bloody way.

Steffan yawns louder than he needs to and stretches, tossing the box into a carrier bag. "Are we going then, or what?"

"Seriously. The plan?" I say. I'm not daft enough to buy this all-about-the-journey bollocks he's trying to sell me. In fact, I'm vaguely insulted that he thinks I'm thick enough to believe it – wrung out and messed up as I might be.

I step between him and the door. "The. Plan."

He looks shifty. "Just, you know, driving... The usual places. All that. A couple of nights, like we talked about..."

"And the rest of it. Come on."

He gives me the same look Amy did. *Fragile*, it says. *Handle with care. Danger: stay back two hundred feet.*

And then he gives up and ruffles his hands through his hair, which he knows makes him look about nine years old, and he meets my gaze and says: "I want to go see Mum. I need to. I just thought, you know, it would be good to do something else too. Go other places on the way. Have some fun. Not make it all about..." He clears his throat again and sticks his hands in his pockets, the way he always does when he's nervous or uncomfortable. Or both.

Ah. I see.

He doesn't need to finish the rest of his sentence. I already know what he didn't want to say. It's not like I can deny him, is it? After all, this is what we do. We hold each other's hands (metaphorically, not literally – god knows where his hands have been...) and we pick each other up. I never thought that hanging out at our respective mothers' graves would become an integral part of our friendship, but life has a way of surprising you. So does death.

He doesn't visit his mother's grave often: her birthday, the anniversary of her death... The usual, I guess. Now is neither of those things, but given the circumstances I can't

31

say it's a shock he wants to go – and while every single fibre of me hates the thought of it, I can't let him go alone. Hasn't he just done the same for me?

"You don't want to go with your dad?" I ask.

"No." His voice hardens, just for a second. He's angry about something, even if he's trying to hide it. There's something going on here. "No," he repeats, more softly.

"Are you…is everything okay?"

"*You're* asking *me* that? After yesterday? Come off it." He grins at me. "I just… Mothers and stuff. You know?"

I do.

# three

"A tent?"

"Where'd you think we were going to be sleeping?"

"I don't *do* camping."

"Bye, then. See you in a few days."

They're enjoying this far too much.

To their credit, they have at least managed to scrounge a couple of tents: the kind that just sort of pop up, provided you put the right tube into the right hole. Or something. As you can tell, I'm an expert.

The last time I went camping, I was five, on holiday with my parents – back in the days when we still did that. Seems like a long time ago. All I can remember is having a plastic baby doll that I liked to bathe in the washing-up bowl. It rained. There was mud. And as we started to drive out of the campsite, my dad (who, thoughtfully, had packed the car the night before and put the inflatable dinghy on the roof rack) tapped the brakes and a tidal wave of rainwater sloshed out of the dinghy and down the windscreen of the car.

Like I said, I don't *do* camping. I know, I know. I should have thought about this more, but I didn't. I mean, it's not like I've had anything else on my mind, is it...?

So. Tents. Tents which are currently rolled or folded, or whatever it is you do with tents to make them go small again, and sitting outside the kitchen door. I'm feeling an attack of The Incompetents coming on.

The Incompetents is that thing you do when you're faced with something you don't really want to try. We've all done it, just to get out of the stuff you probably *could* do – like climbing the rope in gym or, say, putting up a tent – but don't quite have the heart to. And no, before you ask, it's got nothing to do with being a girl: I've seen Arfon Davies come down with a chronic case of The Incompetents at the start of every dissection class in biology for the last year.

Besides, I'm with two great big, lumping boys who just demolished a mountain of bacon, one of whom (Jared) is both taller and considerably stronger than me. (Steffan, not so much, despite how much he likes to pretend otherwise.) The least they can do is put up my bloody tent.

"Fine. Tent. Whatever." It's a couple of nights. It can't be that bad, I think – and all the while I'm trying to forget the opening few scenes of every horror movie I've ever seen.

You know. With the road trip. And the camping. In the woods.

They've already moved on, and are discussing tools. What they should take, whether the car's likely to need some kind of intensive open-engine surgery at the roadside...

Cars feature heavily in any conversation with Jared. Always have, always will, even though he and Steffan didn't pass their tests all that long ago. Jared's been nuts about cars ever since I've known him. Any kind of sport that involves a car, he's into. Racing, rallying, Nascar, the lot. He knows pretty much everything there is to know about cars, too; how they work, how to fix them when they don't. Steffan, bless his little cotton socks, is at the other end of the scale – although it's not for want of trying. Fortunately for him, Jared likes nothing more than having his head stuck in an engine – and Jared's presence is probably the only reason I'm insane enough to get into the rust bucket which passes for Steffan's car.

Except they're out of the door and onto the drive and they're not stopping beside the Rust Bucket. They're still walking, following the curve of the drive around the house and towards the garage. And those keys Steffan's swinging around...they're not his. They're his dad's.

"Uhhh...Steff?"

Ahead of me on the drive, there's the faintest hint of

him slowing down; a suggestion of his head tipping to one side when he hears me. I can guarantee you that he's grinning, even though I can't see it from here. That's not the point: it's not meant for me.

"Steff. Your car? It's back there."

"I know." He flips the keys around his finger again and presses a button on the key fob. There's a *blip-blip* sound, and the garage door rolls open. "We're not taking that one."

His dad's convertible is sitting innocently in the middle of the garage, surrounded by stacked cardboard boxes sealed with packing tape and labelled with fat black marker pen.

*His dad's convertible.*

"You're kidding me."

"Dad said he thinks my car's a piece of crap and this is a bad idea. So we'll be taking his. It's not like he's going to miss it – he left for his golf trip at, like, dawn."

Did I mention that Steffan's…well, rich? Probably not. It doesn't come up much. Not until he does things like this, anyway. You'd never be able to tell from his own car – but that's different. He paid for that himself, so it was the cheapest one he could find that still had all its doors (hence the general crapness). Maybe that's one of the reasons his dad hates it.

Jared's eyes have glazed over, and he takes a step closer to the car. His hand hovers over it for a second as though he's waiting for something, then drops onto the paintwork. He runs his fingers along it like he's stroking a cat.

"The V8. Nice." Both Steffan and I are staring at him. Steffan narrows his eyes. He really does try, but he genuinely knows as much (or as little, depending on how you look at it) about cars as I do.

"It's silver?" he volunteers after an embarrassed pause, and Jared's face creases into a smile.

"It's a good car."

"Yeah, well, I knew that. Even *Limpet* knows that…"

"Oi!" I swat at him, and he laughs.

"Go on then." He waves at the car. He's waiting for me to say something stupid and prove his point – not that he'd know. The only mechanical term Steffan really knows off the top of his head is "Wankel rotary engine" and he only knows that because it makes him laugh.

I shake my head. "Shiny car. Pretty car. Not your car."

"Oh, come on. I'm insured on it. He's not here, is he? He won't even know."

Jared looks up from stroking the car. "Unless you drive it into a hedge," he says pointedly.

It's a long story. And no. I'm not telling.

"Better not crash this one, then, had I?"

In fairness, it was only a *little* crash. Well, little-*ish*.

Steffan looks at me. "Besides, you really want to spend the whole time crammed in the back of the Rust Bucket?"

37

I pause to consider the amount of crap he keeps in the back of his car, and the fact that one of the windows is jammed shut...and the other one only opens halfway. Both of these things had slipped my mind – as they tend to do when you've had a couple of beers, and it's all about the glorious new idea not the practicalities, which are inevitably ankle-deep in old crisp packets. And now there's this other brilliant new idea in front of me – literally sitting in front of me – and I can see us driving down the twisting road that drops down to the beach on one side of the Havens, and I'm stretched out across the back seat in the sunshine with the sea wind in my hair...

"You were saying?" Steffan knows exactly what I'm thinking. Of course he bloody does. "Still want to be The Responsible One?"

"Only if you're going to keep being The Rich One."

He opens his mouth to reply...and closes it again with a small shake of his head. He looks like he's about to say something else...and then changes his mind again. Second-guessing his second guess. That's not like Steffan, who has the worst mind-to-mouth filter I've ever come across. There's a small smile – a sad smile – and then he shrugs. "The so-called Rich One's going to get the bags. Is The Responsible One going to help, or shall I just leave hers in the drive?"

"What's up, petal? You afraid you might not be able to

lift it?" I nudge him with my hip as he squeezes past me and out of the garage.

I'm never sure what Jared makes of the way Steffan and I talk to each other – after all, they've known each other so much longer. Maybe it's a guy thing, but they always seem to dance around each other. Neither of them ever *says* anything. They talk, but you could write down what they actually *say* on the back of a postage stamp; it's all nods of the head and grunts and smacking each other around the shoulder, interspersed with occasional mockery of someone's driving.

I can't talk to Jared the same way I talk to Steffan. With Steffan, it's easy. It's effortless. But with Jared, it's all sharp edges and overthinking and I can feel him watching me when I talk. He's doing it now, from the shadows of the garage. I can feel those eyes of his on my back. He never lets on what he's thinking; just stands there, watching. Weighing. Remembering. Jared *remembers* things; the smallest things, things I couldn't even keep a handle on for a day, never mind a couple of months. But him? He just sucks it all in and locks it away somewhere and you don't even realize until it pops back into a conversation a few weeks later. It's unnerving. He did it to me not long after we met. I'd finished school for the day, and I was waiting for Steffan after rugby practice, watching them head back across the playing field to the changing rooms, when Jared was suddenly behind me, still wearing his kit and covered in mud. "I've got something for you," he said.

"Oh yeah?" What's a girl to say when the new captain of the rugby team hits you with a line like that?

"In my bag. You were saying you liked Hemingway?"

"Was I?"

"A couple of weeks ago. Talking to whatshername. With the bad hair. Outside room five."

That could be most of my English class. "And you were eavesdropping?"

"I was waiting to go into physics. On the steps right across from you. You waved at me, remember?"

"Huh."

"Anyway. I found a Hemingway book of my grandad's in some boxes of my dad's stuff in the attic. Thought you might want it."

"Won't your dad notice it's gone?"

"Not likely. He's not much of a reader. Besides, he's... away a lot."

I already knew about his dad by then. It's a small town, and people talk. People *talk*. It's one of the reasons he changed school: too much talk at his old one. Too many whispers. Too many looks, too many nudges. Not that it's all that different here – everyone still knows, especially in the upper years – but Steffan's got a kind of magic about him, and as soon as the whispers about Jared's dad and who he was and what he'd done started, Steff made it clear they were going to stop. And stop they did. I don't think Jared actually needed Steffan though; after all, once he made the rugby team, he was safe anyway, and as soon as he got switched to captain that was it – he was golden. The rugby team is untouchable. It's an unwritten rule, passed down from on high: you don't mess with the squad. So he may not have needed Steffan, but it's what Steff does. He protects people. He protected Jared; he picked me up and dusted me down and protected me. He still does.

And now, apparently, he nicks his dad's car and takes us along for the ride...

I'm missing something, aren't I? Even by his standards, this is off. I mean, it's not like he ever passes up the chance to wind his dad up, but it's one thing to nick his beer or whatever...and quite another to nick his car.

Steffan's strolling along the drive, whistling, and Jared gives me a look across the garage. He shakes his head and gives the convertible one more thoughtful stroke. Then he sets off after Steffan, who's still swinging the keys around his finger...right up until Jared runs up behind him and snatches them.

There's another *blip-blip*, and the garage door starts to roll closed – with me still inside. It's not elegant, the scramble to get underneath it, but neither of the others notice: they're too busy squabbling over the keys. Steffan has closed his fist around them and is wagging a warning finger with his other hand, and Jared's not having it. Not at all. This continues up the drive... Or at least it does until Jared, with his captain-of-the-rugby-team aim, somehow prises the keys from inside Steffan's fist and lobs them straight into the middle of the garden pond.

Steffan's mouth couldn't drop any further open without his jaw unhinging. He's so shocked that he can't form actual *words*; there's the occasional squeak coming out, but that's about it. He points wildly at the pond, then stares at Jared and, finally, he gets it together enough to shove him away and shout: "You tosser! What the hell's the matter with you?"

"Saving you from yourself, mate," Jared says, blandly. There's a torrent of Welsh in reply, and you don't exactly have to be a speaker to know what Steffan's saying. It's... well, it's not very nice. I wonder how much I miss, not being able to speak it. Probably not much, knowing those two. They both grew up as native speakers...but my parents never saw the point of it. I mean, I had lessons at school like everyone does but I was awful so I dropped it. I pretty much tapped out after "The cat ate my Welsh homework."

As Steffan paces up and down, still swearing under his breath and rubbing at his hair (not to mention coming up with a few brand-new names to call Jared), I lean against the side of the Rust Bucket and try to ignore the groan that comes from its suspension. The picture I had in my mind – the wind in my hair and the sun on my face – evaporates.

Jared winks at me. He's caught it too – that edginess, the sense that there's something our friend, our protector, our fearless ringleader isn't telling us. Still, we're going to have several days in the Rust Bucket. We can always threaten to lock Steffan in until he tells us what it is…

**limpet iPhone / music / playlists / road trip**

Mallory Knox - *Beggars*
Bastille - *Things We Lost in the Fire*
Green Day - *Good Riddance (Time of Your Life)*
You Me At Six - *Lived a Lie*
The First - *Take Courage*
We're No Heroes - *Ghost Coast*
Little Boots - *Remedy*
Fall Out Boy - *Alone Together*
My Chemical Romance - *Summertime*
Super Furry Animals - *Gathering Moss*
Tracy Chapman - *Fast Car*
The Script - *Exit Wounds*
Snow Patrol - *New York*


**limpet iPhone / notes & reminders**

Black dress to dry cleaner's (Amy??)
What's bugging S?
Is J smoking??
Call Amy.
Sunscreen!
Reminder: S dad car keys. Pond!
[Remind me in: ~~1 hour 1 day~~ 1 week]

# four

"You know he's going to kill me, right?" Steffan flicks off the indicator as we pull out of the drive. My foot is sticking to something on the floor behind Jared's seat, and I can only hope it's chewing gum. In this car, it could be anything. I tried to get Steffan to clean it out. I did. I even refused to get in until he cleared the worst of his detritus from the back. When he found the remains of a sandwich in the footwell, I swear I nearly threw up. It was *green*. Bread shouldn't be green. It's just…wrong.

The two of them argued about the car keys while I threw everything in the boot of the Rust Bucket. Picture that, if you will. Them: rugby players. Me: picking up all the bags and loading the car. And they say chivalry's dead. I could hear them, although they were both trying to keep their voices down. Steffan was all disbelief and a filthy temper. Jared was quieter, calmer. He shrugged a lot. That's Jared all over: always watching, waiting, reacting to everyone else (usually Steffan). As they came back over to the car, all I heard was the tail end of their conversation: Steffan saying, "You have no idea what you've just done," and Jared replying with: "It's not like he's not lost his keys before, is it?"

Car keys at the bottom of the pond, or Steffan hurling the shiny speedy car around the B-roads for a couple of days with us in the back. I think we all know which is the lesser of those two evils.

"He'll kill you a lot *less* than he would if you called him from a recovery truck while he's playing golf."

"You think I'd tell him? Christ. No way." Steffan leans into the steering wheel and looks up and down the road, holding the car at a junction as a tractor rumbles past, scattering hay behind it.

"So what, then?" Jared's seat creaks as he slides further down into it, settling in for the journey.

"I'd tell him someone nicked it, wouldn't I?" There's a jerk, and the tyres snicker against the hot tarmac as the car leaps forward and we're away.

You get used to Steffan's driving. It's not that he's bad, exactly – it's that he's…energetic. He throws his car around corners and into bends with complete conviction, and that's probably all well and good if you're up front. But back here? Not so much. The first sharp bend we take, his violin case skids across the back seat and slams into my thigh. It – sorry, *she* (he's adamant she's a she) – is an antique. She cost a small fortune, which came out of his inheritance from his mother. Most of it's locked away until he's twenty-one, but the violin's different. Apart from that, he can't touch it. He doesn't like the phrase "trust fund" but…

Anyway, wherever Steff goes, the violin goes. Even here, even now. And if she keeps bashing into me every time Steffan turns the wheel, *she* and I are going to have a little talk.

It's another unexpected thing about Steffan. You wouldn't think it to look at him: he's a solid-looking guy and he's a flanker on the rugby team, so you'd probably take him for one of nature's brass-players. A trombonist or something. Maybe handy with a tuba. Unfortunately, nature forgot to mention that to Steffan, so he carried right on being a flanker and a violinist. And he's good (at the violin, at least – the rugby's a bit more questionable…). He's really good. The first time I heard him, I wanted to tease him the way you tease friends for being good at things you couldn't ever imagine being able to do – but I couldn't. He's *that* good: he's make-you-stop-and-listen, takes-your-breath-away, too-good-to-take-the-piss-out-of good.

Fortunately, Steffan being Steffan, there's always

something else to take the piss out of him for. What'd be the fun in knowing him otherwise?

Jared has wound down his window as far as it will go and slouched down in his seat. He has his knees pressed against the glovebox and one arm draped out of the car, and he's drumming his thumb and the heel of his hand against the outside of the door in time to the radio, watching the world go by from behind his sunglasses. With a double-tap of his hand, he stops and leans across to whisper something in Steffan's ear. It's the glance back at me that gives it away: he's just realized which road we're on. Steffan's fingers tighten around the steering wheel as he gives himself a mental kicking, but the simple fact of the matter is that the easiest road out of town, the quickest road, the most sensible road, leads right past the graveyard. We're already at the near end of it; I can see the red brick wall and the giant sequoia trees ahead of us and it's as if the last twenty-four hours never happened. In my head, I'm sitting in the back of another car, my black dress creasing in the heat. One glimpse of the gate and I'm transformed into yesterday's me, the one following a coffin.

I can't take my eyes off it. I've driven past this graveyard a hundred – a thousand – times before now, and it's never mattered. Now, though, it's like a black hole with a fresh grave at its heart, and it's sucking me in. My hands are shaking and the back seat of the car is hot and cold all at once and I can't breathe…

"Limpet." Steffan's voice pulls me back to the car, to today, to now, and his eyes meet mine in the rear-view mirror. "You're alright."

"Am I?"

"Sure you are." He glances at the road, then back to me. "You want me to pull over?"

"No! Leave me alone and watch the road, will you?" It comes out louder than I meant it to. More desperate. The last thing I want is for him to stop the car. As long as we're driving, we're moving. I have to keep moving. A single word I overheard Amy say comes back to me – "Treatment…" – and I tell myself that as long as I'm moving, I'll be okay. I'm not running away, after all. I'm running *towards*.

Towards what? Towards something. Anything. Tomorrow. The day after. The day after that. Anything that puts some past between me and yesterday. We're all running, aren't we? Towards, away…it doesn't really matter which.

The red boundary wall is already receding into the distance – although I can't quite stop myself from turning in my seat and craning my neck to watch it disappear around the corner. And before I know it, the wall's gone. The graveyard's gone and it's like the sun has come out

49

from behind a cloud… And the car stinks of cheese and onion.

"You're eating again? Already?"

Jared has a fistful of crisps halfway to his mouth.

"You ate, like, ten minutes ago!"

"Whaf? Mm hungry." Even through a mouthful of dried potato he manages to sound offended.

"You're always hungry, fat boy." Steffan's shaking his head – but he's still looking longingly at the packet of crisps Jared's devouring. "Chuck us one, will you?"

"Not you as well? Seriously?" I slump back in my seat and look for my sunglasses. Last time I saw them, they were disappearing somewhere under the violin case.

There's a crackle of foil as Jared throws a fresh packet of crisps across to Steffan. It lands in his lap. Meanwhile, I'm sure I just spotted the frame of my glasses underneath a magazine on the back seat…

Just as I reach across for them, there's a blast from another vehicle's horn and our car lurches to the right. I'm thrown back into my seat and the side of my head catches the seat-belt bracket. My ear throbs. Steffan's swearing under his breath, eyes wide…and Jared's leaning across the car, one steady hand on the wheel.

"Mate." It's all he says.

Steffan passes the pack of crisps back to him guiltily. "Not such a good idea, maybe."

"No point letting them go to waste..." Jared starts crunching again.

Steffan looks indignant. "How does that work? If I ate as much as you, I'd be the size of a rhino."

"You want to make the horn joke, or shall I?" Jared pulls his sunglasses halfway down his nose and peers over them. But it's not Steffan he's looking at. His eyes meet mine in the rear-view, and he holds my gaze for a second too long... then grins and disappears back behind his shades again. Steffan's too busy focusing on the road to notice, and I'm not sure what just happened.

We turn off the main road and onto a much smaller one, weaving through fields and hedges and woods, and my heart sinks ever so slightly. I know Steffan well enough to know where he's going. Jared shifts uncomfortably in his seat, because he's thinking exactly the same thing. We're headed for the bridge. And on a day like this, with the sun burning a hole in the sky and school a couple of weeks away, we won't be the only ones there.

I don't like the bridge. Well, I say I don't like the bridge, but actually, as a *structure*, as a great lump of stone in the middle of the river, I'm ambivalent about it. It's not what it *is* that bothers me. It's what it *becomes*. Because while it's a bog-standard means of getting from one side of the river to the other for ten months of the year, for the other two it's the centre of what passes for the social whirl round here. It's where everyone goes. Everyone except us.

There's a reason for that.

Steffan likes them more than I do. He certainly likes them more than Jared does. He likes the bridge too. Just like the river is my safe place, I think the bridge is Steff's. It's where his mother used to bring him when he was little. They used to look for conkers round here in the autumn, and in the spring they would lean over the parapet and watch the fish jumping in the water below. Of course he wants to come here on the way to see her. I just wish we didn't have to put up with the company.

As Steffan parks the car up at the side of the road, I can already hear them. God, I can hear Becca's *laugh*. Suddenly, the thought of reliving the funeral is almost appealing. I'd relive it every minute of every day for ever if it meant I'd never have to look at her smug little face again. Maybe it could be *her* funeral? I picture myself reading *her* eulogy. I reckon I could handle that. (Correction: I reckon I could more than handle it. I reckon I could do it with a smile on my face and a song in my heart.)

"Yeah, alright. We're not stopping." Steffan slams his door, and the Rust Bucket vibrates gently. He already knows what we're thinking.

"Not stopping. Because with the parking and the getting

out, it kind of looks like that's exactly what we're doing."
I clamber out of the back.

"You don't have to talk to her, do you?"

"Shame she doesn't seem to feel the same about me then, isn't it?" I don't need to say who I mean. Steffan already knows that too.

"Just...play nice." He has his hands in his pockets as he saunters over to them.


They're sitting on the rocks in the near side of the water, right by the steps down from the bridge. The water's low enough to walk out to the middle without even getting your knees wet – and that's what they've done. There's a couple of empty beer cans in the hollow of one rock, and a pile of cigarette stubs in another. Becca, with her god-awful laugh, is leaning back against Simon, a bottle of something fizzy and neon pink and alcoholic in her hand. And to think I was mocking Jared and his crisps at this time of the morning. Still – that's Becca for you. As if they're trying to prove my point, Simon takes a deep drag on his cigarette, then leans around Becca's shoulder and blows the smoke into her mouth. Jared's eyebrow shoots up, and Steffan makes a loud retching sound. Simon looks up – the cigarette still hanging from his lip – and nods at them. Steff and Jared can get away with doing and saying what they want around him

– Simon's another one on the team, so it all falls under the category of "team bonding", I guess – but Becca's less than impressed. She scowls at them...and then she sees me, and her piggy little eyes light up. She flicks her hair back (only avoiding setting it on fire with Simon's cigarette because he rocks out of the way) and stands up. She's swaying just a touch and I find myself looking at the bottle in her hand. What the hell is that, anyway? Even from where I'm standing, I can smell it. It smells of lollipops; of booze and candyfloss and a total lack of self-respect.

Her eyes slide over me as Simon unfolds himself from the rock and dusts himself down, throwing his dog-end into the river. He hops across the rocks to the bank, grinning at Steffan and Jared. "Alright?" They both nod and make manly noises back. But Becca...she's watching Jared. She's followed her boyfriend and she's standing right next to him, but she's eyeing up Jared, flicking her hair like a demented horse. Unbelievable.

My feelings towards Becca aren't exactly friendly, as you might have guessed, and haven't been since the third day of Year Eight, when she got Rhodri and Mark to empty my bag onto the middle of the school field and spend the next ten minutes kicking my books around. Where was I? I was right there, learning the hard way that people lie and that not everyone who claims to be your friend stays that way. And how did I know it was her, that she was the one behind it? Easy. She was the one holding me back as they did it, laughing as my stuff got covered in mud.

She sniffs and takes another swig from her bottle of what I fervently hope is a new and exciting poison as she steps towards me. "I saw your dad in the shop last week. He looked kind of shit."

"Yeah, well. His wife had just died, so there's that, isn't there?"

She's just that little bit too close to me for comfort, and I'd like to step back – to put more space between us – but I won't. Because that would be backing down.

"Still, on the plus side? At least there's fewer bottles to be carrying home now." She smiles sweetly as she says it – so sweetly that it takes me precisely three seconds to decide that I'm going to punch her in the face. So I do.

I can't tell who's more shocked: her or me. She staggers backwards, squealing and clutching her hands to her cheek, dropping the bottle. Violently pink bubbles spill out of it, and I'm honestly surprised they don't start eating into the rock. My hand hurts, and there's a buzzing in my ears and I am going to take her to *pieces*. Not just for the crack about my mother. Not just for that day in Year Eight. Not just for the thousand and one snitty little comments made barely loud enough for me to hear over the last few years. But for every single time I've turned my back on her and walked away. And, boy, does *my hand hurt*.

Becca is shrieking…something at me. The problem is that she seems to have reached a pitch that only dogs can hear, so all I'm getting is a high whining sound. She's shrieking and she's about to throw herself at me, and I think I'm yelling back at her only I'm not sure I'm actually in control any longer and I haven't a clue what I'm saying – and then there's Jared between us and Steffan behind me with his hands on my shoulders, pulling me back. Simon's got his fingers so tightly wrapped around Becca's shoulders that his nails have turned white, and by the set of his jaw I can see I've not made myself popular, but there's nothing he can do.

The buzzing in my ears drowns everything else out. I'm sure Steffan's talking to me, but I can't quite pick out the words he's using as he tries to steer me away from the river and back towards the road. Jared's pointing at Becca; his mouth's moving, but it's all white noise to me…

Already, the side of Becca's nose and cheek are starting to swell.

My hand hurts, and yes – it was worth it.

"You're lucky you didn't get her nose – you'd have broken your hand." Steffan's walking me away from the bridge – not to the car, but up towards the fields. "How's it feel?"

"Good. Really good." My heart is pounding. I feel like I've just jumped off a high cliff and managed to land on my feet.

"Your hand, thicko. How's it feel?" He stops walking me along and takes my hand, stretching the fingers out and curling them back into a fist. It hurts, but not as much as it could. He frowns, then bends my hand around a few more times, making me wince (probably for his own amusement rather than anything else), before letting it drop.

"Tell me, doctor. Will I ever play the violin again?" I raise my other hand to my forehead melodramatically.

"Piss off, you." He cuffs me around the back of the head as Jared catches up with us.

"I wouldn't do that," says Jared, obviously trying not to laugh. "Haven't you seen the right hook she's got on her?"

They're mocking me. And yeah, I know, I deserve this one – and they're not going to let me forget it. Not for the next twenty or so years, anyway. After all, what are friends for?

# *five*

"You want to talk about what just happened with Becca?"

"Do I ever want to talk about Becca?"

We're sitting up at the top of the hill by the old pillbox, looking down towards the river. The fort used to be part of a prisoner of war camp during the Second World War: they brought captured Italian soldiers to this area. Most of them worked on the farms, and the story goes that a lot of them stayed when they were released – married and settled down here. God knows why. All that's left of the camp now is the old church and a couple of beaten-up concrete bunkers and watchtowers like this one. I used to think they were the ruins of a fairy-tale castle and every time we drove past, I'd press my nose up against the car window and try to imagine knights riding up and down the valley in shining armour, or princesses sitting in tower windows and combing out their hair. The reality? Italian POWs, shovelling cow shit. Awesome.

The three of us are leaning against the largest remaining chunk of concrete. The sun's on my face and it's quiet and the air's full of the dusty scent of hot summer grass. You can see for miles over the trees, out across the fields. The cars on the bypass look like tiny glittering fish in a river from where we're sitting, catching the sunlight as they dart along the road. You can see them, but you can't hear them this far away. We're too high up. All you can hear are the birds and the occasional cow. It feels like we own the world. Of course, if we actually *did* own the world, I'd have had something a hell of a lot more unpleasant done to Becca. It would probably involve pliers. Rusty ones.

The pain in my hand's settled into a gentle throb. Who knew that walloping someone round the face hurts you as much as it does them? I suppose it's karma. Either that or the fact that if you smack two sets of bones together, both of them are probably going to smart a bit...

I hope Becca's face hurts as much as my hand does. In fact, I hope it hurts more. It bloody well should.

"So, you don't want to talk about it?"

"No. I don't want to talk about it. You want to talk about what's going on with you?"

Steffan jerks away from me, but Jared's on the other side of him, watching expectantly.

"Nothing's going on with me." Steff stares at the ground, picking at a piece of grass.

Jared doesn't believe him any more than I do, and says as much. But with more swearing.

There's silence. Jared and me watching Steffan watching us. He's looking from one of us to the other, and I can tell from his eyes that he knows he's been busted. He's still trying not to spill, though. "Seriously. There's nothing going on."

Jared shakes his head. "So all this stuff. The car. The cigars. That's nothing."

"And you'd know a lot about it, would you?" Steff shoots back.

"I'm just saying…"

Cigars. So that's what's in the box. If Steffan's taken his father's precious cigars then, yes, there's a problem. Or there will be when his dad gets back from his golf trip. He paid an obscene amount of money for them, from what Steff's said.

Steffan picks at the grass some more, and pulls the head off a daisy. "It's not a good time." A shadow flickers across us: a buzzard, wheeling overhead, riding the thermals.

"Is that right?" Jared leans his head back against the hot concrete and closes his eyes. He looks like he doesn't care, like it doesn't bother him whether Steff talks or not. He *looks* like it doesn't bother him either way. Doesn't mean it's true.

This is, as usual, where I come in. "It's never a good time. That's kind of the point, isn't it? I thought that's why we're here. Because it's not a good time for any of us right now. It's not a good time, and it should be – and it isn't fair." There it is. My little voice drifting up to the heavens, saying those three words I've been trying so hard not to say. *It's not fair.*

It's not fair. It's not fair.

It's not fair that I have to deal with Becca – and everyone like her, with their small-mind, small-town whispers and their sideways glances.

It's not fair that I've had to watch my family fall apart while I stand there and do nothing, because what else could I do?

It's not fair that the summer – the time when I'm supposed to be on the beach or in the park or just staying up all night for the hell of going to bed as the sun comes up, when I'm supposed to be thinking about the future, *my* future – has been turned into my own private hell where I leaf through coffin catalogues like I'm picking out curtains or colleges.

It's not fair that it couldn't be in six years. Six months.

It's not fair that it's now.

And it's not fair that this is how I think, that I resent something so sad, that on top of everything else I feel guilty – and it makes me feel even worse.

Somewhere, there's a little cloud of it's-not-fairs, just waiting to rain on me. Which isn't fair either. So it goes.

My it's-not-fair approach seems to have worked though, because finally, *finally,* Steffan's shoulders droop a little and he sags back against the wall. "We're moving. How's that for not fair?"

"*What?*" He gets it in stereo as we both say it at the same time.

"Dad's been headhunted. Something about an advisory role in a blah-blah-blah. I wasn't really listening."

"You're *moving*? When?"

There's a studied silence. He won't look at either of us.

"When, Steffan?"

"Three weeks."

"*Three weeks?*" I've gone shrill. I hate being shrill. Jared's doing that half-smile-that-isn't-really-a-smile thing, shaking his head. Now *he's* picking at the grass. Right now, though, it's Steffan I'm interested in. "And when were you going to bring this up?"

"Dunno." He flicks a ladybird off his knee. "First there was *his* dad" – he jerks his head towards Jared – "and all his family shit, and then there was..."

"My family shit."

"Well, yeah." He shrugs. He's worried he's offended me with that, but I'm not offended. I'm shocked, if anything. Shocked that he's kept this to himself; that he didn't feel he

62

could tell either of us. It's huge. The kind of thing you tell people. The kind of thing you tell your friends. Mind you... thinking back over the last couple of weeks it's all pretty huge, and none of it in a good way. I can't help but wonder whether we've upset some great cosmic balance – and that's even before I punched Becca.

"Three weeks. But you've not been packing or anything."

*Cardboard boxes in the garage...*

"It's part of the deal; they send people to do it all for you."

"Steff..." Jared looks thoughtful. "That's a relocation package. One of Mum's lot got offered that a few years ago, and that was the end of them." He peers over his sunglasses. "Where *exactly* are you moving to?"

"Yeah. About that."

"Where?"

"LA."

*There's always Steffan. Always has been, always will be.*

*Or maybe not.*

I'd been expecting him to say Cardiff. Bristol. London. Somewhere that wasn't the other side of the world. I mean, even in London we could still see him sometimes; catch a train maybe. Get the coach. But America? That's crazy.

"But...what about school?" My voice is shaky.

"It's all taken care of. They've got me a school place... somewhere, and then Dad wants me to apply to music college. Thornton, or something."

"Is that what *you* want, though?"

"Does it matter?" He scowls and bites his lip.

"Of course it matters! Why are you letting him do this? He can't!"

"He can, alright? It's complicated."

"How complicated can it be? It's your life, isn't it? Don't you get a say?" I'm indignant for him, I think; he's so calm. Too calm...or maybe he's just pretending to be. Steffan, our protector, is protecting us again. He's already had this conversation, hasn't he? He's had it over and over again: just him and his dad, with no one there to speak up for him. No one to make his father see that this isn't what he wants, but he'll take what he's given because it's easier, and that's what you do when it's you against them and there's no one in your corner.

His mother would have been in his corner.

And that's why he wants to visit her grave. He wants to say goodbye...again.

Oh, Steffan.

She baked. It was what she did, Steffan's mum. She didn't like cake (or so she said) but she loved baking, and their house always smelled of whatever had just come out of the oven. There was a downside to this: she liked to *experiment*. She'd order flavours from all over the internet. I've still not forgotten her peppermint and rose sponge – it was...unique. Even Steffan turned his nose up at that one, which tells you just how bad it really was. But she was always smiling and laughing, and there was always music in their house and flowers in the garden, even when she was sick. And then she died.

You never see the really big things coming, do you?


Jared has gone very quiet. Which is going to make our little expedition fun, isn't it? He's giving Steffan the silent treatment. Steffan's...well, not *quite* all there. And I'm a shambles. Maybe we should just turn around and give up on the whole thing.

I don't even blame him – Jared, I mean. And I don't think his reaction is just because he's known Steffan even longer than I have. They started primary school together on the same day and they were in the same class for years, until Steffan went to the school where he'd meet me (and where Jared followed a bit later). They've been in and out of each other's houses since long before I came on the scene, so to Jared, losing Steffan must be like losing part of his past. But there's more to it than that, and I wonder if it has something to do with Jared's map.

The first time I went in Jared's room, I saw the map on his wall; big enough to take up all the space between his bed and his window, marked with pins and bits of string and pictures torn from magazines. I thought it was kind of weird, but it was Steffan who explained it, of course, as we wandered back down the street that evening in the early autumn sunshine. Apparently, Jared always said that as soon as he was old enough, he was going to leave. Just go. He'd get the cheapest flight he could to the East Coast and work his way across the States until he wound up in California.

"Then what?" I'd asked. Steffan just shrugged and kicked a stone down the pavement.

"I don't think he's thought that far ahead. It's just what he's always wanted to do."

Of course he hadn't thought ahead. He hadn't thought about passports or visas or Green Cards or…anything. Because that's the one thing about Jared that people don't realize. He's smart and he's on the rugby team and he's good at maths – but he doesn't just *look* like one of those old movie stars. He *thinks* like one too. Even after all the things that have happened with his dad (or maybe *because* of them), he's kind of innocent. Sweet. He's…what do you call it? Naive? That. He's like the kid who grew up on a farm, wearing dungarees and slinging hay bales… And now he's got *me* talking like we're in an old movie and everyone's about to break into a song about how sunny it is and how there are flowers in the hedgerows or something. Anyway, you wouldn't believe all this if you saw him take down the St Matthew's team centre at the last match – but that's Jared for you. A mystery. A riddle. He's The Quiet One. He watches and he listens; less forgetful than I am, less self-absorbed than Steffan. It's like he's always waiting for something – a chance to make a run for it, maybe.

I look at him looking at Steffan again and I catch it; it's only there for a second, flashing across his face and disappearing in a heartbeat, but it's there. He's jealous. Steffan's taking Jared's escape plan…and he doesn't even want it. The wrong one of us is going to America and we're all as trapped as each other. All stuck in lives that are determined by other people. Other people's choices. Other people's mistakes.

Steffan puffs out a long, slow breath and throws the middle of a daisy at me. The white petals are scattered around his knees. "Still," he says, dangerously close to smiling at me, "I bet that's taken your mind off your hand."

"It had. Until you brought it up again. Thanks for that."

"What? You think you're going to be allowed to forget that one? Just wait till school starts and Becca kicks off again."

I hadn't thought of that. School, without Steffan. *Becca* without Steffan.

How much can one person take? I wonder. How much can we carry before we break? How much more for Jared, with Marcus and his mother and now his dad back again? How much more for me? Becca's comment was cruel and it was meant to cut...and how many more will there be? How much can we take, and how much more can we lose?

Steffan knows I'm thinking it. He's thinking it too. "We're pretty screwed up, aren't we?"

I laugh. "Speak for yourself. I'm perfectly adjusted."

"Yeah, right." He dusts his knees off and clambers to his feet. "*Adjusted*."

"That's all I've got, I'm afraid."

"That's all any of us have got." He smiles at me, and I grin back.

Jared shakes his head at the two of us. "You two are mentals, you know that?"

Steffan throws his arm around my shoulder and I lean into him. We both pull faces at Jared, who shakes his head again and laughs as he hauls himself to his feet and rubs bits of grass from his hands.

They're ready to move on. They're probably right. Places to go, things to see, people to...

On second thought, maybe it's better if we *don't* bump into anybody else for a while. Either way, we've got to find somewhere to camp tonight before night actually rolls around.

Steffan tosses his car keys to Jared, who snatches them out of the air without even breaking his stride.

"Spock, you have the conn," he says, and Jared rolls his eyes.

"The original series? Really? Like I said: mental."

"Listen, mate, Kirk was cocking *amazing*."

"And you're Kirk, clearly." Jared pockets the keys. This is an old argument and we all know how it plays out, but they do it anyway. Who'd have believed that the pair of them are closet *Star Trek* nerds? Or that they'd have sucked me into it too? Honestly.

"Bang right I am. And you..." He raises his hand, thumb extended and fingers splayed in the Vulcan salute as he pulls a mock-serious face and raises an eyebrow.

It's my turn. "You're both rubbish."

"Oh yeah?"

"Yeah. Bones is the best. It's always Bones." I shoot them a grin back over my shoulder. "The reboot version of Bones, obviously."

And, predictable as the moon rising, the tide turning and the clouds bursting on the one day you've not got an umbrella, I can feel them thinking it. If I turn around, they'll have the same soppy look on their faces that they always do, and they say it in chorus.

"Uhura."

Like I said: *predictable*.

# six

Mothers. Our mothers. Steffan's baked. Jared's is…best left out of the discussion.

Mine?

Mine likes…*liked*…to control things. Events. People. She was the one who *did* everything, organized stuff and ran things. When I was little, she always said it was because that's what she was trained to do, what she'd learned in her management course at college, and it was just easier for her to do everything. As I got older, it changed to being because nobody else could do it as well as she could. We're talking about the small stuff: Sunday family get-togethers, barbecues. Dinners – not for thirty or forty people or heads of state, but for a couple of my parents' friends. People who had never cared whether the bookshelves in the hall were dusty, and never would…but she still spent three days getting everything perfect for them.

Gradually, it started to wear her down. I didn't see it at the time, and maybe I should have. But you kind of assume your parents are...well, your parents. They're the ones in charge, right? They remind you of it often enough, so it must be true. They've got it all worked out. You're the one who's stuck figuring out how the world fits together and what the hell you're going to do in it, and why you shouldn't be so terrified of the thought that it sets your teeth on edge. They've already *had* their turn.

I wrote my mother's eulogy at three a.m. and I told myself it was just like any other piece of homework I've ever been given. But it wasn't. How do you catch someone in words? How can you trap a complete soul in a handful of pages and bring them back to life in front of the people who've known them their whole lives? People who know them as someone *else*. I only ever knew my mother as my mother...but they knew her long before she became that. How do you tell them who she was and not lie? How can you?

One way or another, everyone lies at funerals.

Jared has spent a good five minutes adjusting the driver's seat and we're still parked by the bridge. (Thankfully, alone now. Because Becca'd love this.) Five minutes. I've watched as the hands on my watch ticked round. Five minutes of shuffling the seat one click forward, two clicks back. Twiddling the cracked plastic dial on the side of the seat to tip it forwards and back. The Rust Bucket being what it is, most of the car's held together with hope, faith and chewing gum, so when it's fiddled with too much, the seat mechanism has a strop and bangs the whole thing back onto my knees right as I'm sliding across the back seat.

"Oi!" I shout and Steffan glances over his shoulder at me from the passenger seat as Jared sighs and yanks his chair forward again.

"Remember: not my fault," Steff says pointedly.

"It's your bloody car," I snap.

"And who wanted to bring it? Hmm? We could've—"

"No. We couldn't." Jared's finally happy with the seat. And now he's started on the steering wheel.

I do not remember a time when I wasn't stuck in the back of this car in the hot sun – a car, I might add, with no air con and with windows that barely work – waiting for Jared to be ready. Eons have passed. When they find me, I'll be nothing but a pile of dust, still waiting in the back seat.

Dust to dust.

I know.

Suddenly, it comes to me. The sunroof. There's a sunroof. It's closed. Hot air rises, doesn't it? So if I open it, the car can't possibly get any hotter. It'll get cooler, because of physics. Or something. Not even the Rust Bucket can argue with physics. Of course, getting to the handle is going to be tricky, but the pair of them are too busy bickering about the sun visors to listen to me…

I slide forward as best I can and lean in between the seats, twisting around so I can reach the handle. That's how old this car is – no electric sunroof here. Like I said: hope, faith and chewing gum. Steffan looks up, poking me in the ribs as I grab the handle. It turns and the roof creaks open and suddenly there's fresh air on my face, and I'm looking up at clear blue sky framed by green leaves. It looks so blue you could dive into it.

It's not elegant, but I twist some more and manage to stretch far enough to poke my head out through the sunroof. It's just wide enough, I think… I wriggle, and my shoulders scrape up through the hole too.

"What the…?" Jared's finally noticed what I'm doing.

"It's boiling in there!" I don't know whether he hears me. I don't care. The sky is sapphire and the breeze is on my face…and the engine starts.

I'm not rushing for them. I wriggle my arms through the gap and rest them on the roof. My palms tingle on the hot metal.

"Would you sit down already? I get it, okay?" Steffan's getting antsy. I'm still not rushing. The air tastes different here. Up by the pillbox, it tasted of summer and parched grass and hot stone. Here, back by the river and without

Becca to spoil it, it tastes clean and clear – although that might be because the car still smells of cheese and onion crisps, with a hint of banana going off in the heat. I knew I should have made Steffan check under the seats.

I'm just about to slide myself back into the car when I hear the click, and then the groan of the suspension...and the car creeps forward.

They wouldn't.

Would they?

The car keeps on creeping. It pulls away from the side of the road.

They would. They have.

Bastards.

The breeze picks up as the car moves – still slowly – along the road. There's no traffic here; past the bridge and surrounded by the fields and the trees, there's no one left to see me but the ghosts of POWs. We pass the memorial at the crossroads and I feel the breeze pick up and the wind tug at my hair, and without knowing why I'm doing it, I throw open my arms and close my eyes and I'm flying.

"Faster!" I shout down to Jared, but I can hear him telling me to get back inside.

"You've had your fun, Lim. Sit down."

"No!"

"I'm not kidding! Sit your arse back down, would you?"

The car sweeps to the left, then back to the right. It's

gentle, but deliberate. I take the hint and slide myself back in through the sunroof, dropping into my seat. Jared's fingers are gripping the steering wheel and even behind his sunglasses I know he's frowning.

"You could have just waited, you know," I say.

Steffan's pale when he swivels in his seat to stare at me. "What was that?" he asks.

"Forgetting," I say, and fasten my seat belt.

# *seven*

The boys are learning that pop-up tents don't actually pop up. I did warn them about this when they were yammering on about how easy it was all going to be and wasn't the whole "camping" idea so amazing. I think they were expecting to just unzip the bags and a tent to magically appear out of each one, all ready to go. Ha. But you can't tell them – really, you can't. So I've been sitting here on this tree stump for the last twenty minutes, while they wave a bunch of metal rods around and get tangled up in a load of fabric, generally getting themselves into a hell of a mess. They also seem to have invented a couple of brand-new swear words. They're surprisingly original.

We've driven a while, and they've argued over which station to tune the car radio to (not that it matters because, round here, it all disintegrates into static and white noise every few minutes anyway). And Jared has complained about the Rust Bucket's clutch a grand total of forty-three times. I counted.

There are bags piled up on the ground beside them. The Rust Bucket's a few minutes' walk back through trees and a couple of fields, parked in a lane where it won't get in anybody's way. Basically: the arse-end of nowhere.

"Better get used to roughing it, Lim," Steffan had laughed as Jared turned off the ignition.

"You're not serious."

"Course I am. The great outdoors, isn't it? Sleeping under the stars…"

"Naff off."

"Cooking food over a campfire. Washing in the river…"

"You're definitely not serious."

"Says who?" He'd blinked at me with such sincerity that he had me believing him.

The horror. It was only when his face crumpled and he burst out laughing, shaking his head and saying "Your face!" over and over again that I realized he was messing with me.

"I hate you both." I tried not to pout. "When you said 'camping', I kind of pictured an actual…campsite. Some of them have shower blocks. Some of them even have – shocker – *pools*."

Steffan shook his head. "Round here. In this weather. Like there'd be anywhere with space in the summer holidays."

Jared snorted. "And like anywhere would let us in."

Fair point.

He carries on. "See that shed over there?" He pointed through the windscreen to a low, white-painted building squatting at the far side of the nearest field. "That's the St Jude's changing rooms. And over there?" He pointed the other way. "A mile or so down the road, there's a pub. No cooking over a campfire. Promise."

Everyone knows what happened at St Jude's. At the start of the year, the young PE teacher got accused of…well, doing something he shouldn't have been doing with a Year Ten pupil in the changing rooms after a football match. Needless to say, he didn't stay a teacher at St Jude's very long. I don't know what happened to the kid, but the teacher was gone pretty sharpish and no one's seen him since. That's the thing about small towns and reputations. They're like tinder, dry as anything – it only takes a single spark, and before you know it the whole forest's burning. Anyone who's ever lived in a town like ours could tell you that.

The upshot of this particular conflagration, however, is that the St Jude's changing room building no longer has ⸺ on its front door…

"You're a genius!" I said as I figured it out. No lock means that a hot shower is there for the taking.

"Not so hateful now, is it?" Steffan grinned. He's not quite right; it's just that I'll probably hate them less after a shower.


"You're holding it upside down."

"Bollocks I am."

"Might as well be holding those, all the good it's doing you," Jared mutters out of the side of his mouth at Steffan, who makes a rude gesture with the rod he's holding.

I'm bored. And I tell them so.

"How can you be bored?" Jared peers at me over the top of the instruction sheet. "Here, surrounded by the glory of nature…" He waves his arms around as if to make a point.

From my tree stump, I peer past him at the clearing in the middle of a crappy little collection of trees that is our campsite for the night.

"The glory of nature? Since when has the glory of nature included an empty wine bottle, three rusty lager cans and…" I squint, just to make sure. "An upside-down shopping trolley sitting in the river? And how the hell did that get all the way out here, anyway? Who'd be so determined to dump a trolley in this *particular* spot that they'd haul it through a load of woods?"

"Who knows why anyone does anything round here?" Taking advantage of the fact that Jared's distracted, Steffan snatches the instruction sheet out of his hand and scowls at it. "You dipstick. You're telling me I've got the bloody pole upside down – you've got the whole sheet upside down, haven't you?" He waves it in front of Jared's face.

"Was it?"

"Yes. Did those funny shapes that looked a bit like upside-down capital letters not give it away?"

"Is that what those are? Huh." Jared doesn't look impressed. He looks even less impressed by my attempt to hide my laugh as Steffan continues to call him a long list of exciting names.

"You realize it'll be dark soon, right?" I'm exaggerating slightly. It's not going to be dark for a while yet – not even at the rate they're going – but if I say I'm bored again, I'll sound like a four year old. Instead, I stand up and dust my jeans down. "I'm going to go over to St Jude's to take a look at the changing rooms."

"Let us know if the water's on, yeah?" Steffan barely looks up from the tent. He's now picked up a handful of the fabric and is stabbing at it with one of the tent poles. Either he's finally worked out how it's supposed to fit together or he's attempting to sabotage Jared's chances of staying dry if it rains. It could go either way.

I leave them to it and start picking my way through the trees and back towards the St Jude's playing field.

There's a hole in the front of the door where the lock used to be, and it takes little more than a nudge to open it. So that's all fine – but it's pretty dark inside. Changing rooms being what they are, you don't exactly get big picture windows down the side of them, do you? There is, however, a light switch just inside the door, which I find by fumbling around like an idiot.

Naturally, it doesn't do anything. I flip it up and down several times, because *obviously* faith healing is going to work on a broken light switch.

Still nothing happens. I have failed in my attempt to miraculously fix the lights. I'm going to have to look for some kind of fuse box, aren't I?

Armed with my one "practical science" lesson from Year Eight (when Mrs Dalston handed everyone in the room a plug and a screwdriver and a handful of clipped wires and told us to put them together, before sitting back down at her desk to glare at us) I'm going to try and turn on the electrics in the St Jude's changing rooms. This can only end well, right?

Right.

The changing room block sits right on the edge of the

school's fixtures field. They've got another field too, next to school, that they use for their PE lessons. But this is the posh one – the one for playing other schools. Which is nuts because it means that everyone hates St Jude's matches. Even the St Jude's teams. *Especially* the St Jude's teams. Think about it: it's the middle of January, you've missed your whole lunchtime to run around a freezing cold pitch for an hour, getting the full benefit of the horizontal rain... and when you're done, you get changed and cleaned up in what's basically a concrete shed. After all that, you have to trudge back out into the cold and the mud and the sideways rain and get soaked again on the ten-minute walk back to school...where you spend the rest of the day dripping gently into your shoes. As an exercise in building team spirit, it's really something. Shame St Jude's still suck at rugby anyway – and the less said about their hockey squad the better. Even *we* usually beat them at hockey.

The grass is longer around the side of the block; left uncut since the start of the summer, it reaches to my knees and the seeds stick to my jeans as I walk through it looking for a fuse box. I don't know why I've assumed that whatever it is that controls the electricity is outside, other than because if it is inside, in the dark, I don't stand a chance of finding it anyway. And I want my shower; I can feel the dust sticking to the sweat on my face, just sitting there, and now there's going to be a lovely thick layer of pollen or whatever it is that's kicking up out of the grass too. So yes. Shower.

My foot hits something solid hidden in the grass – something solid which clinks. An empty bottle. A collection of them, actually: vodka bottles. The cheap type that the local offies always have sitting beside the till with *Special Offer!!!* written on neon cardboard stars stuck to the front. There's also a couple of crumpled-up cigarette packets and a pile of dog-ends. So not only are they a classy bunch here at St Jude's, they're a cliché with it.

Something glitters in the grass next to the bottles – and I take a step back. That's not glass. It's metal. It's a needle. It's sticking straight up, invisible until the light hits it – and I almost trod right on it.

The sunshine doesn't feel as warm any more, and with a shiver I realize that I'm out here in the middle of a field, alone. My phone is in my bag – which, naturally, is still in the pile next to Jared and Steffan.

It's fine. I'm fine. There was no one around me a minute ago, and there's no one here now. Nothing's changed. It's just…that's a needle. A needle, you know? Outside a school changing room. Would it have been sharp enough to go through the thin sole of my flip-flop if I'd taken that one extra step? And if it had…what then?

It dawns on me that – lights or not – there's no way I'm going into that changing block on my own.

The walk back across the field feels very long and, although I should know better, the *what ifs* start piling up. Even though I know there's no one there, I keep turning around to look behind me as though I'm expecting to see someone standing by the changing block, watching me walk away.

They're still bickering. Of course they are. But now, at least, one of the tents is up. It's a little wonky, and it creeps a couple of metres backwards when the breeze picks up. (Because who bothers with something as boring as pegging a tent down? I mean, *really*? Not Steffan, that's for sure.) But it's up. Well, up-*ish*. Only two more to go.

"So? What's it like? As shitty as usual?" Steffan barely looks up from the rod he's trying to unfold.

"Yeah. No. I didn't go in. The lights wouldn't work."

"You scared of the dark all of a sudden?" He means it as a joke, but between his lips and my ears the words somehow twist and become something else.

I've never been afraid of the dark. Not even when I was little. The dark was comfortable and it was quiet, and I always understood that there are no monsters just waiting for someone to throw a switch and set them free. The world doesn't change around us simply because the lights go out. *We* change.

I never was afraid of the dark…but lately it's got noisy. The darkness is no longer quiet and it's no longer empty. It's loud and it's full. Full of doubt. Could I have changed anything? Was there anything I could have done that would have made a difference? Is there any way I could have ended up not watching them carrying my mother's coffin into that church? *What if, what if, what if?* I don't know. In the light, I tell myself there's nothing that I could have done; that it wasn't my fault. People make their own choices and live their own lives and then they die. That's how the world works.

In the light, that's what I tell myself.

But in the dark…

Jared glances up from unfolding the fabric of the next tent, and there must be something about my expression which catches his eye, because he stops unfolding and he straightens up and the grin fades from his face.

"Shut up, Steff." He takes a swipe at Steffan's arm, making him look up, then turns back to me. "What's the matter?"

"It's nothing. I just…" I run my hand through my hair, brushing it away from my face. This isn't a thing. It's not. It's just me getting freaked out because I almost stood on some junkie's needle. It's fine.

I'm easily freaked out these days. I keep feeling like I'm resting on a knife-edge: one nudge and I'll tip completely over into…something else, some*one* else. I've been told it's shock, it's normal, it'll pass. But when? When do I get to go back to being me? The old me, the me who started the school holidays? Her life might not have been perfect, but I'm not asking for *perfect*. I'm asking for me. That's all. When do I get to be her again? When will *this* – this other person who has taken my place – when will she pass? She and I, we're not the same person. We're not the same and I'd like her to leave now.

I try again. "It's nothing. It's stupid, honestly. There was just this pile of rubbish round the back and there was a needle in it and I almost stepped on it. It was kind of...you know?" I tail off. Saying it out loud doesn't exactly make it sound any *less* stupid.

"A needle?" Jared's eyebrows go up. "What's that doing there?"

"Oh, come on," Steffan laughs. "It's St Jude's. Wouldn't you be more surprised if there wasn't one?" But then he looks at me and turns serious. "You're sure you didn't *actually* tread on anything though, right?"

"*Now* you're concerned?"

"Piss off, then." He grins and shakes his head and goes back to the tent – and I'm half-grinning too. Freak-out officially over.

Jared lets the tent fabric drop to the ground and rubs his hands together. "Bet you a tenner they've turned off the electrics for the summer."

"Well, yeah. Even I'd got that far..."

"And you'd know how to turn them back on, would you?"

"Can't be that hard, can it?" I sound more sure about this than I feel.

"How about I come with you this time, and I'll turn them back on."

"And I can't manage because I'm a girl. Is that it?"

Steffan snorts. "Don't be thick. It's because you can barely even work a toaster. Christ knows what you'd do to yourself turning on a circuit."

Jared, however, just smiles and shrugs. "Offer's there."

How can I refuse?

Principles are all well and good...but I really, *really* want a shower.

# eight

Trailing over the field behind Jared, I find myself wondering whether things would be going this way if the trip had happened a week ago. I correct myself as a small but insistent chime goes off in the back of my head. Three weeks ago, then; would this have happened three weeks ago? Three months? A year? Have things between the two of us changed because my mother died; because his mother suddenly sees his dad's release as her own – a release from being a parent?

I am a cracked glass. Set me down too hard and I will shatter into a thousand jagged pieces. Knock me and I will cut. "Crazed" – that's the word, isn't it? Is that what I am now? Am I crazed?

My mother always used to put broken glasses in the bin, wrapped up in sheets of newspaper so that no one would get hurt. Am I like those glasses – fractured, useless – or can I be mended? Is it too late? After all, people have already been hurt. But that wasn't my fault. That was hers. She drank and she died and I'm just the damage that's left behind. The chipped glass left when all of the bottles have been cleared away. Empty.

Ahead of me, Jared's feet crunch in the dry grass. It crinkles under the soles of his trainers. He's looking off somewhere towards the end of the field – at the changing rooms, probably. The sun's lower in the sky now and somehow it makes the little block look menacing, standing there all alone. Like something from a horror movie. Two of us go in…but I'm the protagonist, right? I mean, this is all about me, so surely I'm safe? The odds aren't exactly in Jared's favour though, are they?

"Do you think he's alright?" Jared's voice snaps me out of my thoughts. I have no idea whether he said anything before that, but there's only one person he can be talking about and that's Steffan.

"I guess." That and a non-committal shrug are the best I can do. Steffan's Steffan, and even if something feels off now, I've never known him not be alright. Well. Alright in the end, anyway.

"The shit with his dad's car…"

"To be fair, he's always done that kind of thing, hasn't he? You know what he's like." And it's true. He has. Like I said, Steffan's Steffan. Somehow, he always manages to be the centre of attention – even when he's not actually there.

"What about you?" I ask. Although it's not so much asking as panting, since I'm having to take half-skipping steps to try and keep up with Jared. I never noticed how fast he walks.

"Me? What about me?"

"With your dad and…stuff."

"It's not a thing." He's shutting me down, isn't he? Or at least he's trying to. I recognize it because it's my new way of life: fake normal and hope it sticks. Pretend you're okay and people treat you like you are. It's only if they suspect you're not that the sympathy voices come out. If you move fast enough, nobody ever sees the bruises.

"Not a thing?" I manage to get in front of him. He stops – reluctantly – and stares at a spot somewhere just behind me. "How is it not a thing? If it was me—"

"But it's not, is it? It's not your life. It's mine. And that's just what it is. Life."

"I'm just trying to—"

"I know." His eyes snap up to meet mine. They lock on to my gaze and hold it, and it's like I'm looking at a statue. His face is that quiet, that cold. "Back off, would you, Lim?" There's an edge to his voice.

I could keep pushing. Jared's the stillest, calmest guy I've ever met – and when he *does* lose it (which is rare) he gets even quieter. I've found a sore spot and I can't help but want to worry at it, worry *about* it. I've always had this theory that if only you could find the cracks in the wall, you could bring it down completely and see who Jared is inside. I could push. I *could*.

I think of all the "And how are you really?"s, the "It's the least we could do"s and the endless questions asked with kind smiles and empty eyes which I've faced over the last two weeks, and I decide not to push. If there's something he's keeping to himself, it's for a reason.

Honestly, him and Steffan are as bad as each other.

We reach the changing block and Jared disappears off round the back, being very careful where he puts his feet. There's a clattering noise and a small amount of swearing and then his head appears around the corner.

"Anything?" he says.

"How the hell am I supposed to know?"

"Try a light switch, maybe?"

"There's no way on god's green earth that I'm going in there by myself. There could be...junkies or axe murderers or...or..." I'm flapping. I'm flapping and he's grinning at me.

"Axe murderers. Plural. Sure – like one isn't unlikely enough?"

"You never know. It's always the quiet towns, isn't it?"

"And even though you're convinced there are multiple psychos in there, you're happy to send me in."

I think about this for a second, then nod. "Yes."

He rolls his eyes at me, then steps in through the main door.

It takes a minute or two but then there's a click followed by a buzzing sound as the lights flicker on.

Jared's one of the good ones – despite everything. Maybe *because* of everything. I don't know; you'd think that having that much chaos around him (his dad in jail and his mother being about as much use as a fish lighting a bonfire) would screw him up in the head, wouldn't you? But I wonder whether that's the reason he is the way he is; having been treated like shit most of his life, it makes him not want to treat people the same. Maybe he's just, you know, A Good Guy.

There's a squeak which sounds like a shower tap being turned, and then an ominous clanking sound…and then a sort of spattery-whoosh.

My shower! I can't believe I'm quite so excited about something so incredibly boring – but between the hot car and the trees and the grass, I feel like I've grown another skin. A grimy, sticky, sweaty skin. One I'm looking forward to shedding.

There's another sound from inside the changing block…and suddenly all my worries about junkies / axe murderers / weirdos who want to wear our faces as hats come flooding back. It's a big, heavy sound like someone being thrown around.

"Jared?"

Why am I standing here like an idiot? The lights are on. Why am I still outside while he's probably being dismembered by a family of zombie devil-worshippers?

It comes again – a great big crashing thump of a sound – and I decide I can't just leave him to be savaged by a mummy or eaten by…whatever it is. Something with big teeth.

"Jared?" My voice bounces off the white tiles as I step inside. "You in here?"

"Don't be thick, Lim. Where else would I be?" The voice comes from just behind my right ear. So I do what I do best in these circumstances, which is squeal loudly and emphatically, and leap in the air. Because I am *all* the cool.

The look on Jared's face tells me he's not even slightly surprised by all this.

He's holding out a towel.

I look at him. He looks at me.

He looks at me, and my heart's suddenly in my throat. And it's not just the whole undead-mummy axe-murderer thing. It's something *else*.

"I found the towel locker," he says, still holding the towel out.

I'm supposed to take the towel, aren't I?

Like I said: *all the cool*.

"So that's what the racket was." I take the towel. Finally. Well done, Limpet.

"Seeing as you don't seem to have brought one over here with you, I thought you could probably do with a towel. And the locker was, as the name implies, locked."

"Until you came along and broke it with your man-arms, is that it?"

"Piss off." He grins and shakes his head at me. "Thought you were desperate for a shower. So why are you standing there giving me a load of grief?"

"I'm waiting for you to *go*, obviously."

"That's it, is it? You use me, then you—"

"*Out!*"


I am pathetically grateful for my shower. Say what you like about St Jude's (and we do – we really, really do) but they've made my day. The towel's a little like sandpaper, and the weird shampoo-and-bodywash-combo bolted to the wall smells a bit, well, funky, but I'm clean and that can only count as A Good Thing. Shame I also forgot to bring a comb, which means that I'm going to have comedy hair. There's no point in fighting it: I can feel it drying as I get dressed. I run my fingers through it a couple of times but there's really no point. It is what it is. And at least it's clean. Ish.

The air smells cooler when I step out, and there's a hint of smoke, like a reminder that summer's almost done. I'm not sure I'll miss the summer; not this one, anyway.

Jared is leaning against the wall outside the door. I'm a little surprised to see him; I thought he'd gone back to supervise Steffan, and my face clearly says that before I even open my mouth.

He just shrugs. "No lock on the door, is there?" he says. "Thought I should hang around, just in case. Axe murderers, right?"

See? One of the good ones.

# nine

The sun's starting to haze by the time we get back to our little campsite: it's almost too late to call it evening any more, but not quite properly into night yet, and the sky is that shade of orangey-yellowy-pink that lasts for all of five minutes and then it's gone. As we walk in silence through the field (if you don't count the other noises: birds calling to one another, the last of the day's bees – dirty stop-outs, the lot of them – cars on the road, every tractor in a fifteen-mile radius suddenly out and about in a last-ditch attempt to get the hay in, the river, just on the edge of hearing…the countryside's noisier than you think) Jared's face is lit in bronze. The setting sun's rays catch in his hair and make it glitter. His eyelashes look like they're made of gold and I swear you could see his freckles from the other side of the field. He's still a statue, but now he *glows*.

Me? I've got sticky-up hair and one of my flip-flops is starting to rub. Natch.

Neither of us speaks. There isn't much to say, is there? It's like all the banter in the changing block took the last bit of energy we both had and now everything's sharp and uneven again. I can tell that Jared is a good guy – I can. It's just that...he's like someone carved from stone, cast in clay, but watching you with living eyes. Watching and remembering – but not judging, not this time. Of all people, Jared knows what it's like to be judged – worse, he knows what it's like to be judged for what someone else has done. And he's got to go through it all over again when his dad comes home. There'll be the same whispers as always.

I don't know who hears it first: Jared stops walking sooner, but my hearing's usually better than his.

It's music.

It's a violin.

It's Steffan.

He's playing the violin and it's beautiful, carrying on the evening air like it belongs there. Like you could breathe it in, swim in it. Drown in it.

I told you he was good.

"Guess this means he's sorted the tents then," says Jared.

"That or given up on them," I say, rubbing my toes against the back of my calf. The walk across the field has already speckled my feet with grit and broken grass stalks.

Steffan can play anything; he only has to hear a piece of music once and he can replicate it. "Perfect pitch," he says. Incredibly annoying, I say – like the time he spent three weeks playing that stupid jingle from a car advert just because he could, and because he knew it drove everybody else crazy. He only stopped when I threatened to take his bow and…well, yeah. He stopped.

I don't recognize what he's playing now. It could be anything, I guess, but there's something sad about it. He's playing fast and the notes pour out from between the trees until they're almost on top of one another – and yet again I wonder how it is that he can do that. How can someone so irritatingly normal be so special? Because he *is* special, even I can see that.

Maybe this move, this music school, will be the best thing that ever happened to him. Maybe in twenty years, when he's rich and famous, he'll look back and say that it was all because his father moved him across the world. And maybe it will be. But all I can think about is how he's being taken away from me when I need him more than I've ever needed him. And if that makes me selfish, then so what? Is that so bad, wanting to keep someone? Isn't it bad enough that I just lost one person, and now I have to lose another? That I get the same say in this that I had in my mother's death? And at that moment, with the music dancing around me and the sun sinking behind the hedges, I realize I'm thinking about him like he's going to die. That's how this feels: as concrete and as heavy as death.

He doesn't look like someone about to die. Which is reassuring, because he isn't. In fact, he looks like he's been busy; obviously Jared was being less helpful than he thought. The disastrous tents I left in favour of a shower have all been straightened and put up properly; they've even been pegged down in a rough triangle, with what looks like the makings of a campfire in the middle. He's also found a couple of chunks of tree trunk and dragged them into the middle of the clearing, arranging them round the little firepit like benches. He's pacing up and down behind the furthest one as he plays and he barely notices us as we walk out of the trees. He isn't playing for us, after all. He's not even playing for himself. He's just *playing*.

He'll play until he stops. There's no other way of putting it: it's like he's in a trance and he just has to get the music out of him. He'll pace up and down and even though his eyes are open he won't really be seeing anything and all he'll hear is the notes. There is nothing else when he does this. There's only him and his violin.

He'll be back in the world of the living sooner or later, and in the meantime, I think I've found the bag with the crisps in.

* * *

Dinner is tepid chips, which Steffan has managed to get from the pub up the road, while, from the drinks menu, Sir has opted for the house special: body-temperature beer, the bottles still warm to the touch even now the sun's gone down.

As soon as he stopped playing, Steffan made sure we told him how clever he was for managing to put up the tents without losing either a finger or his temper, and reminded both of us that, yes, he did go to Scouts for a while as a kid and he's really not as hopeless as we seem to assume, despite all evidence to the contrary. I managed to cover my laugh at that with a sort of hiccup, but Jared didn't even try. Steffan threw a stick at him across the clearing. He missed.

Jared is the one who gets the fire going, pulling a lighter out of his pocket.

"Why've you got that?" I ask, peeling the label off my beer. It's sticky and clings to my fingers.

"For lighting campfires," he says with his back to me. I glance at Steffan, who raises an eyebrow and shrugs before reaching for a new bottle.

"Bollocks. Since when do you smoke?"

"Who says I smoke?" Jared sits back on his heels and blows gently into the beginnings of the fire. If I wasn't so startled by the lighter's sudden appearance, I might even be impressed.

"Nobody carries a lighter if they don't smoke, do they?"

Steffan swallows his beer with a loud gulp. "My granddad used to. It's how he met Nan – he lit her cigarette."

"So, basically, he carried a lighter as a pickup?"

"Well, yeah."

"But your granddad was a nutter."

Steffan ticks his head from side to side. "Not always. I mean, he *was*, but that was something to do with the cancer getting into his brain and shit."

He takes another gulp. Oh, Steff. His granddad died of cancer a year to the day before his mum was diagnosed. Sometimes you can't help but wonder whether the world's just laughing at you.

"So, Jared suddenly whipping a lighter out of his pocket means he's on the pull, does it? Looks like it's your lucky night, sweetheart!" I wink at Steffan over the top of my beer bottle. He pulls a face.

Jared pretends he's not heard any of it and scoots back to his tree trunk as the fire takes hold of the sticks and little branches he's piled into the circle of stones – and I remember that faint scent of smoke earlier. I'd gone all poetic and thought it was something to do with autumn moving in (or, at the very least, a local farmer burning a load of crap he shouldn't be) but Jared sneaking a cigarette seems just as likely.

It's funny how things like this remind you how little you

really know about your friends. I mean, you spend all this time together at school, at weekends – even doing stuff like this – but how much do you ever know somebody? How much do they keep locked away in a little box, just beneath the surface of their skin? All the walls, all the masks, all those lines of defence, they get in the way.

"Any other secrets you'd like to share, Jared?" Steffan asks.

Jared shakes his head. "Wouldn't be secrets then, would they?"

"Gambling problem? Drug habit…?" Steffan's eyes flick to his drink as he skips over the obvious one for my sake. Of course he does.

"How'd you find out? I play online poker to finance my crack habit. That's when I'm not busy dismembering hitch-hikers and selling their body parts on the black market."

"Thought you ate them?"

"Cannibalism's so over, don't you think?"

By this point, even I can't keep a straight face any longer. We're still all laughing when my phone chirps with a voicemail – probably from my aunt. I promised I'd call (there's another one who's smoking on the quiet – what is it with everyone?) and, as usual, I've forgotten. The fact she's actually left a voicemail means she wants to talk. Now.

Even I'll admit that I'm bad at checking my voicemails. It's a habit I got into because of my mother. She used to call my phone, and it would be at the bottom of my bag so I didn't hear it or get to it in time, and she'd always leave a voicemail. And it was always exactly the same: "Hello. It's your mother. Please call me back." If I didn't call her back within the next five minutes then there'd be another beep and another message left with the same weary tone. "It's your mother again. You haven't called me back." And so it would go on – never mind the fact that if I actually tried to call her back, her line would be busy because she was leaving me yet another bloody voicemail.

Come to think of it, why did she always start off with "It's your mother"? Like I wouldn't recognize her voice?

Trying to ignore the other two (who are now busily discussing which bits of a person would be best to barbecue – I'm not sure I'll ever be able to face barbecued ribs again) I dial Amy. There's no answer. I think about leaving a message, but don't. Instead I hang up, dial my voicemail and listen to hers.

It's not what she says that bothers me; that's all just the usual how-are-you-where-are-you-what-are-you-doing? kind of thing, asking me to check in. It's the way her voice sounds: thin and pulled too tight. She's worried about something – and it's not me. She'd come out and tell me if it was me. So it's something else. There are strange sounds in the background – too muffled for me to hear them properly. It sounds like shouting. Like something heavy being thrown.

I listen to the message twice more – and by now the others are watching me. Waiting.

Three listens in, I still can't tell for sure who's shouting or why. But I can make a pretty good guess.

It's my dad, isn't it?

No wonder she was keen for me to get away from the house.

Poor Amy.

I'm about to hang up from my voicemail when a little robotic voice chimes in. "Next message," it says. And just like that, I freeze.

Whatever I'm feeling, it must show on my face, because Steffan is on his feet and across the space between us before I can process the first words that come out of my phone's little speaker.

"Hello. It's your—" And then my phone is ripped from my hand. Steffan's darting away from me, clutching it, pressing the keys, and without knowing what I'm doing or why, I'm going after him. At least, I'm trying to – but Jared's arms are around my waist, holding me back.

I can hear myself shouting. I can't make it stop. I can't make any of it stop. I can't make Jared let go and I can't stop screaming and I can't stop Steffan from deleting my mother's voice for ever.

Jared's grip is strong, and it's only when he releases me that I can move. Steffan is already holding my phone out to me apologetically. I ignore it, and slap him across the cheek as hard as I can. It hurts my palm; but it's a different kind of pain to when I hit Becca (who am I? I never used to be this, to do this; to lash out like a feral cat). The slap hurts Steffan's cheek more than it hurts me though; already I can see a shocking imprint of my fingers spreading across one side of his face, as though I'd dipped my hand into red ink and painted the image onto him. He drops my phone and I snatch it up before he can reach for it, clutching it to me like a newborn kitten. I try my voicemail and my hands are shaking so hard that I can barely hit the right key.

"You have no messages."

How I hate Voicemail Robot Lady, and how I hate Steffan. The force of it surprises me as it washes over me, rushes through me.

"You had no right," is all I can say.

He hasn't moved.

"No right." I sound like an echo of myself.

"I know."

He isn't even trying to apologize. He knows he can't, that there's nothing he can say that will make what he just did right. But I know there's more coming. He opens another beer and he sits. And he talks.

"When Mum died, I saved the last couple of messages she'd left on my voicemail. It's not like they were special or anything; one of them was her having a right go at me for being out late one night, and the other was her going mental because I'd not done...*something*. I listened to them every fricking night for three months, Lim, just to hear her voice. And you know what? The more I listened to them, the worse it got. Maybe because I *knew* that those were the last things I'd hear her say – ever – and maybe because in both of those stupid messages, she was disappointed. She'd left them because of what I'd done or not done or whatever. I'd let her down. Every time I listened to them, that's all they reminded me of. Letting her down." He sets the bottle down between his feet and lowers his head into his hands. I can see his fingers working themselves through his hair until he looks up again and he looks me straight in the eye. "You don't want a disappointed voicemail to be the thing you remember."

"How do you know? How do you know it would be disappointed?" My voice is thick. It doesn't sound like mine.

"You tell me, Lim. Honestly. Did she ever leave you any other kind?"

He picks up his beer again. Jared is frozen between us, and the only sound is the fire crackling.

I can't look at either of them any more. Not Steffan, for what he's done, and not Jared, for not letting me stop him.

"I'm going to bed."

My bag's already in my tent. I zip the entrance closed

behind me and lie down on the thin foam mattress and I close my eyes, because no one can really cry with their eyes screwed shut and if I don't cry then it doesn't hurt. It can't.

There's an owl out there somewhere, and I can hear it hooting nearby. Calling to its own kind. It's peaceful. Soothing. At least, it's soothing if you're not a mouse or a shrew or any of the other small furry things that are about to become its dinner...

I can hear the others moving about outside the tent, probably getting ready to turn in for the night themselves. I feel momentarily guilty: I guess I put a bit of a damper on the evening. Well done me. There's a hissing sound as one of them throws water on the fire, and Steffan coughs.

They're very quiet by their standards, quieter than they should be, and it's not because they think I'm going to sleep or anything. If they wanted to make a racket, they'd make one regardless of who I was or what I was doing. I catch the odd word of Welsh – mostly Steffan, but sometimes Jared. They're talking about something, talking quietly like it's a thing that shouldn't be discussed in the open. Like it's a secret. Even though I can't understand what they're actually saying, I understand the tones of their voices well enough, and Jared's not happy. Neither of them are, not really. However cheery they seemed in the day, the night has brought something else out of them.

I'm still listening to the murmur of their voices and wondering what it is they don't want me to know as I drift off into sleep.

**limpet's iPhone / music / playlists / road trip**

Taylor Swift - *I Knew You Were Trouble*
The Killers - *Mr. Brightside*
Mallory Knox - *Death Rattle*
The Heavy - *How You Like Me Now?*
Catatonia - *International Velvet*
Stereophonics - *Local Boy in the Photograph*
Foo Fighters - *Learn to Fly*
will.i.am feat. Skylar Grey - *Love Bullets*
Ella Henderson - *Glow*
5 Seconds of Summer - *Amnesia*
The Vamps - *Wild Heart*
Avicii - *Wake Me Up*

**limpet's iPhone / notes & reminders**

Charge phone in car.
Beach!
Kick S till he bleeds, because bastard...
Never sleep in tent again. Ever.
J's dad?
Call Amy!!!

# *ten*

I sleep better than I have done for weeks, even though I'm in a tent in a scrappy little bit of woodland in the middle of nowhere and my neck aches and I've obviously been lying on an entire fallen tree the whole time. Still the best sleep I've had in a while. When I woke in the night once or twice, all I could hear was the river, and someone snoring. My money's on Steffan.

But the sound that wakes me in the morning? That's not snoring. That's…

My ears are telling me I know that sound. I know what it is, and it shouldn't be here. I shouldn't be hearing *that* out *here*. No way. Scrabbling for the zip to the tent, I shake the last of the sleep from my head and – ever graceful – half climb, half fall out into the daylight. Jared and Steffan have obviously done the same thing, and as I dust myself off and straighten up, we stare at each other.

"You heard that too, right?"

"Well, yeah."

"So I'm not losing my mind? Good."

"*Losing?* Ha!"

"Funny."

And then everything stops, because there's the sound again – and it is very, very definitely being made by an elephant.

We stare at each other some more.

"That's insane," says Steffan.

"That can't be real," says Jared.

"Where do you think it's coming from?" I ask – and the two of them are frowning at me. "What?"

Maybe they're waiting to see whether I'm still angry with Steffan. I am, I suppose, but he's my friend. You get angry with friends, don't you? That's kind of the whole point: that you get angry, and they understand why and you move on – and they try not to be such a dickhead in future. Or something. And they don't ever, ever touch your phone again; not if they want that hand to be able to touch anything else afterwards.

What's the point in dwelling on it, anyway? He deleted a voicemail. He was trying (in his tactless, hopeless, usual bloody way) to help – and for that alone I guess I have to forgive him. After all, if anyone understands the way I feel now, it's him – although sometimes, I *do* wonder…

But you push on, don't you? It's not worth losing a friend over. Nothing is. Not a friend like this; a friend like him.

They're still frowning.

"You want to go find the elephant." He thinks he's humouring me. I'll show him.

"Listen to what you just said, Jared. It's an elephant. An *elephant*. Here. We're not exactly tripping over exotic animals roaming the woods of west Wales, are we?"

Steffan mutters something about "town on a Saturday night."

We both ignore him.

"It's not real," says Jared, bluntly.

"Okay, so why, for the love of god, would someone pretend to be an elephant all the way out here where there's no one to even hear them?"

"Well, there's us." Steffan shrugs. "We heard it."

"Exactly. Wait. No. What was I saying? No. Never mind. Come *on*. Aren't you even curious? At all?"

They answer almost simultaneously: "Not really," says one. "Nah," says the other.

"You're crap. The pair of you. Where are your balls?"

"Look who's talking," Steffan says with a barely disguised snigger.

I thump his arm. "Oi! What's that supposed to mean?"

Somewhere in the back of his head, a little alarm bell apparently starts ringing. I can see him very carefully considering what to say next – just in case he triggers what he only semi-affectionately refers to as "the femrage". This is the charming nickname he's come up with to describe the look on my face when I've caught him being…well, a bloke. It's a fairly loose category which includes (but is not limited to) making smutty comments and whispering to Jared in Welsh whenever one of the Year Thirteen girls walks past the common room. Like I don't know him well enough to know *exactly* what he's saying. And don't even get me started on the wallpaper on his computer. Seriously.

Finally, Steffan decides he's figured out a way through the minefield. "Didn't you need Jared to go hold your hand in the changing room because of the scary, scary druggies who left a load of crap around?"

I'm going to let it go – purely because he was as worried about it as I was. He's teasing me. It's his way of checking whether normal service has been resumed, or whether I'm going to try and punch him in the kidney the second he turns his back. Tempting as that may be, it's not really in line with my whole "friends" policy. More fool me.

"Whatever. *Elephant.*"

The elephant in the woods trumps everything.


We leave the tents where they are for now; there's nothing much in there to steal and none of us can be bothered to take them down yet. Besides, it's bad enough that Steffan insists on taking the violin back to the car and hiding it under a load of junk in the boot. I don't want to wait any longer. Because, you know, *elephant*.

I say we're out in the middle of nowhere. Technically speaking, for round here at least, that's not strictly true. There's the pub, a couple of villages within ten minutes' drive, a handful of farms, and of course there's the St Jude's field. Like I say, by the standard of things round here, we're practically in the suburbs. Years ago, the woods had a reputation for attracting stoners looking for mushrooms – and the reputation's stuck, judging by the needle I almost trod on. So maybe there is something weird going on out here.

The ground is parched and dusty, even in the shadow of the trees; the summer's taken no prisoners. Big cracks criss-cross the soil where tree roots have pushed up close to the surface, and brown leaves, their edges curled, skitter about in what passes for a breeze. They're thicker on the ground than usual at this time of year – even the oldest trees are struggling in the heat. And when we get close, the river's lower than I've ever seen it. Shopping trolley and all.

"You want to try crossing?" Steffan scowls at the water, like that'll make any difference.

"It's shallow enough."

"You first, is it?"

"Coward."

"Manners. Ladies always go first, I thought." He winks at me. He's waiting for me to fall over and land on my arse in the middle of the river. Of course he is.

"Well, *fine.*" As I pick up my shoes, I congratulate myself on wearing shorts today – not that they could save me from getting wet, of course; it just feels like this way I'll be somewhere closer to the "dignified idiot" end of the sliding scale than the "total loser" end.

The water's cooler than I was expecting. After the first shock of it, it's nice. The riverbed here is mostly flat rock, worn smooth by the rush of the water, and it feels almost soft beneath my feet. Something solid, moving, brushes my toe. "Just a fish, just a fish, just a fish," I whisper to myself. Not a monster. Definitely not any kind of monster, and an axe murderer would have a hell of a time hiding in this little water. Besides, how do you swim holding an axe? (Answer: carefully.)

I can feel their eyes on my back the whole way across – so when I make it to the other bank without having slipped, splashed, tripped over my own toes or otherwise embarrassed myself, I'm feeling more than a little smug. "Ta-daa!" I shout back at them. I bow. They roll their eyes.

"Yeah, alright. Bravo. You walked in a straight line and you didn't fall over." Steffan is not as impressed as he ought to be, frankly.

"Ah, correction: I *forded a river* and didn't fall over. *Totally* different thing."

"Christ, you're annoying." He's strung his shoes together by their laces around his neck, as though he's wading across the Amazon. As he sloshes through the water, they swing to and fro and smack into his chest with every step. Jared – thoughtful as always – follows him across, carrying his trainers and peeling off his T-shirt to dry his feet when he reaches the other side. The sunlight, dappled through the moving leaves above us, dances across his bare shoulders. There's a scattering of freckles just below his collarbone – and before I can stop the thought, I imagine my fingertip tracing the line of them over his skin; feeling the warmth of his chest beneath my touch.

I boot the thought out of my head as fast as I can – but what if it shows on my face? He's got his trainers back on now and he's standing up, wriggling back into his T-shirt. What if he looks at me? Will he know what I was thinking? Do *I* know what I was thinking – was that even me? I mean…it's *Jared*, right?

"Bloody tart." It's Steffan, sitting on the ground and trying to work his still-wet foot back into his trainer. It's taken him till now to get the laces unknotted. "Whipping his top off left, right and centre. Any excuse." He shakes his head. Jared just smirks.

I'm safe.

It takes Steff a very, very, very long time to get his hobbit-feet back into his shoes. "Right, then," he says finally, standing up and brushing himself down. It's exactly the same thing his dad does: the gesture, even the intonation of his voice. Steffan probably has no idea. I wonder whether we all copy our parents in one way or another. Are their mannerisms built into our bones, or do we just catch them after years spent in close proximity? Can you catch a gesture, a turn of phrase, like a cold – or are they already coded into our genes? And what about the other things: taste in music, in books? Favourite foods? Tics and bad habits. Diseases…and addictions. What about those?

The trees are thinner on this side of the river. Less wild – not that the woods across the river are particularly wild. After all, they belong to someone, don't they? Here, though, they seem…neater, somehow. As though somebody wanted to keep them that way. And there's the beginnings of a path, by the look of it. Are we about to just go tromping into the middle of someone's garden? There's only one place I can think of this far into any woods round here, and surely we can't be…

The path suddenly deposits us onto a sweeping driveway winding through the trees – once it was gravel by the look of it, but now it's mostly dust and potholes.

"Oh, no," says Jared from behind me. When I look round,

he's rubbing his face. He knows where we are. He drops his hand, and shoots me an anguished look.

I know where we are too. And suddenly, I understand the elephant in the woods.

This is Barley Vale.

I had no idea we were so close to it – although I probably should have twigged as soon as I heard the noise this morning. Any other time, I probably would have. I wonder whether Steffan realized; it's painfully obvious that Jared didn't. I guess we've all just got other stuff on our minds.

It used to have a different name, this place, until a handful of locals complained that it was "out of keeping with the area" – for which you can usually read: "'s *foreign*, isn't it, and we don't like foreign" – so Barley Vale is what it became. The sky-blue railings and the slightly ramshackle collection of Portakabins and breeze-block buildings in front of us, all painted white with peeling red guttering, and the agricultural shed behind them, looming out of the trees, is all that is left of the hospice. Somewhere behind them, set into the side of the hill, must be the temple.

Just like everybody knows the story about the mushrooms, everybody knows the story of Barley Vale. How it started as a beaten-up old shed used by a couple of hippies, and then turned into a commune. Somehow, a guru got wind of the place and moved in, building a small hospice for the terminally sick and spiritually inclined, and a temple. The hospice turned into a bigger hospice, the temple turned into two temples and a visitor centre and kitchen, as well as a hostel for pilgrims who came to see Guru and pray at the temples.

Oh, and there was the elephant. According to the local papers, it was rescued as a baby by Guru from...somewhere, and brought to live at the Vale. They built the barn for him to sleep in, and there were rumours about him following Guru around like a puppy and being taken for walks in the woods on a lead.

Barley Vale was where some people came to live and some came to die. Some were just passing through on their way to somewhere else. Until it went bankrupt.

Which brings me back to Jared – standing in the middle of the ruins of his father's biggest con.

# eleven

I know what you're thinking. What kind of man steals from a hospice – a hospice with a temple and a guru and an elephant, no less?

I'll tell you what kind of man.

Jared's father.

I can't remember whether the fraud was why he went to prison the time before last, or the time before that. There was an assault in there somewhere, but I don't know if he actually did time for it. The latest conviction was the really spectacular one: for attempted murder. It was the first time where Jared refused to visit him inside – which may or may not have had something to do with it also being the first time Jared had sat in the gallery in court. He was old enough to hear it all by then – all the things his grandparents and even his mother had tried to protect him from. He heard it all and with it he heard everything that had gone before.

I can't imagine how that must have felt.

The rule with Jared's dad – with Jared all over, I guess – is that we don't ask. Not Steffan, not me. Not really. It's part of the roles we've built for ourselves over the years: the Rich One, the Quiet One, the Responsible One Who Is Prone To The Occasional Outburst Of Drama. The names are only part of it. We owe it to him not to ask the big questions, because the answers are messy and painful and will force him to dig up things he's long since buried. And besides, neither of us want to ask those questions, because all they would do is push Jared back into the box of his relationship with his dad – someone who's been gone more than half Jared's life anyway. Someone who doesn't know the first thing about what makes him laugh, or what his lopsided squinting-frown means (that he doesn't approve), or anything more significant than what his favourite football team used to be when he was five.

No, don't ask me. It's sport, isn't it? I don't do sport.

Barley Vale was one of Jared's father's scam victims – along with most of the town. He stole from more people than he didn't, and he didn't discriminate and he showed no mercy. Everyone was fair game – even this place. Nobody knows where the money went, but it sure as hell went. The hospice was the first to shut down, for obvious reasons. The little community there just couldn't keep it running. The monks managed to keep the hostel running a little longer, but that money ran out pretty fast…and gradually, everybody left. Now, all that's here is a bunch of rotting buildings and a rusty tin shed.

And, apparently, an elephant. You'd think somebody would notice that, wouldn't you?

The big barn is to the side of the cluster of buildings. Jared hangs back, looking around him as though he's trying to picture everything as it was before. It's hard. The concrete steps going up to the doorways are cracked and chipped, with straggly grass growing out of them. There are big ruts in the drive where wheels sank into the mud at some point, now long-dried by the hot summer. Sheets of dust blow across the driveway, chased by a few curled brown leaves. Steffan slaps his hand on one of the railings and the metal rings out in the silence, making me twitch. It reminds me uncomfortably of a funeral bell. He's looking at his palm, and pulls a face: the blue paint has flaked all over his skin. He brushes his hands together, but instead of the flakes coming off, they simply spread to cover *both* his palms.

"Can we go?" Jared's voice is low.

"But—"

"Lim, I can't be here."

"Why?" I turn to face him properly.

"You know why." He won't meet my eye. Steffan's rubbing his hands together furiously, utterly oblivious. Maybe a little too oblivious.

122

"Because your dad did this?" I wave at the emptiness. It breaks my heart – both the desolation in his face and in the deserted space. There's a shrivelled brown bush in the corner of the yard that I think used to be a rose. Now it's just a dead weed. "You're not responsible for him, for what he does. Don't you dare think you are, Jared."

"He ripped all those people off – all *these* people off." His wave mirrors mine, but just like a reflection, they mean different things.

"Exactly. *He* did that. Not you. You're his kid, not his keeper. You are never responsible for your parents' actions, Jared. Never."

"Neither are you." This time, he looks straight into my eyes; straight into *me*. And he holds my gaze and I hold his, and I could almost swear—

"Looks like we're not the only people here," says Steffan – and I tear my eyes away from Jared's to see a man in cut-off denims and a faded orange T-shirt rounding the corner of the yard. He doesn't look thrilled to see us, but on the other hand he's not brandishing a shotgun, either. (You laugh, but it's not funny when it happens. Honestly, we were only taking a short cut back across the field. Talk about an overreaction...)

"Lost, are you?" he calls, scratching his head. He's watching us carefully.

"Nah." Steffan's the one who answers.

Whatever it was that passed between Jared and me, he missed it. And there was *something*, wasn't there? I don't think I imagined it. There was.

Steff nods back towards the river; towards the car and the campsite and a time, only seconds before, when I knew exactly where I stood. "We're from town, you know? Camping. Heard the..."

"You want to meet Piggy?" The man's suddenly all smiles.

"Piggy?"

"Come round. He loves company." And with that, he vanishes back round the corner.

Steffan blinks. "Piggy? They called the elephant Piggy?"

"Well, they called *you* Steffan," Jared says with a shrug as he slides past me without even a second glance.

I don't know what the hell is going on any more.


There are some things, I've learned, that manage to take you completely by surprise no matter how you think they're going to go. Sometimes it's good, sometimes it's bad... sometimes it's just different. This is one of the Just Different times.

There, in the middle of a shed which was only really designed to hold cattle, is a small elephant. Piggy. He looks pretty happy to see the random guy we've just bumped into, and I realize that this must be who's taking care of him. After all, someone has to feed him, don't they? And muck out his shed. But there's no way Random Dude is a zookeeper, or even remotely qualified to look after something like an elephant – little or not. In fact, I'm almost certain I've seen him around town on market days, which would make him one of the local farmboys and would probably mean that the closest he's ever been to any kind of exotic animal would be if he had a pet budgerigar when he was a kid.

He answers my question before I've even asked it, leaning over the pathetically flimsy metal barrier – again, meant for sheep, cows, the occasional pig at a push... "They're trying to find a zoo for him. Had a couple of the keepers from Cardiff come and spend a few days down here when the place went under, have a good look at him. They can't take him, but at least they gave me a few pointers to tide us over. The RSPCA pop in, but it's a bit out of their league, really. I heard the lot in London are keen – and apparently there's some Russian fella after him for his daughter's sixteenth birthday." He shakes his head at the idea. "It's a whole different world, isn't it?"

Piggy the elephant scuffs at the straw on the floor of his barn with a foot the size of a dinner plate. Steffan eyes him carefully.

"What if he, you know, goes psycho? They do that, don't

they? I saw a thing about it once." A half-hour documentary on when elephants attack is, in Steffan's eyes, enough to make you an expert on the subject.

"Then we'll have a problem, won't we?" Random Dude shakes his head again. "I tell you what, there's no way I'm chasing him through the woods if he gets out. No thank you. I'll feed him and that, but I told them I'm not responsible for him, no."

When I glance over at him, Jared's eyes are like ice – cold and bright as I've ever seen them as he watches Piggy – which is just marvellous, really, because now on top of everything else, Jared apparently feels responsible for an elephant's imminent nervous breakdown.

I thought I wanted to see this, but I don't. I can't bear the sight of it. The poor thing is stuck here, with no choice but to stay put and wait for someone to want it. Everything about it is wrong – even its name. Piggy. Who calls an elephant Piggy? Trapped by his name, trapped by his circumstance…just trapped.

I feel like if I don't leave now, I never will.

Steffan's obviously feeling the same. He catches my eye and nudges Jared, who snaps out of his daze. There's something about Steff's expression, though; something in the way he's looking at Jared. Something I don't recognize, something so strange and unfamiliar and so not like *him*…

"Listen, d'you mind if we take a look around before we go?" Jared asks the guy.

Random Dude ticks his head from side to side. "All the same to me either way. Watch, mind – some of the buildings are a bit dodgy these days. Guru never was very into health and safety." He says it with a laugh that suggests he approves. Which wouldn't surprise me: most of the farms here have been in the same families for generations, and they like to do things the way they like – even if that means fixing the radiator of a tractor with gaffer tape and a bit of string (and yes, I've seen worse than that driving along the back roads). Being a bit cavalier about maintenance is seen as a badge of pride.

Random Dude and Piggy have lost interest in us, so that's that. Thank god. A depressed elephant is not what I had in mind for today. But what I want to know is why Jared suddenly doesn't want to just get the hell out of Dodge.

"Because I want to see it. While we're here. I want to see what he's done."

"But what for?" I ask.

"So that one day, I can tell him that I've been here. I can tell him how much damage he's done." Jared's voice is measured and calm; so measured and calm that few people besides us would be able to tell just how angry he really is. I can count on my fingers the number of times I've seen him get angry, and I can count the number of times I've seen him actually lose his temper on just one.

Once. That's it.

Steffan, his mood apparently improved, is balancing on the lower bar of a set of railings (he's also seen a couple of shows about parkour – naturally, this makes him not only an authority on it but a world-class practitioner; I give it two minutes before he lands on his head) and listening to Jared impassively. When he finishes, Steff coughs and says: "Mate, why don't you just tell him he's a wanker and leave it at that? He couldn't exactly argue with you, could he?"

Jared appears to be considering this...and then, just like that, his scowl cracks into a grin and he laughs. "Fair point. I'll keep that as my backup."

The clouds that were gathering clear away, and suddenly I feel better. And I realize that it wasn't this place that was making me feel so edgy, it was Jared's mood. It infected us all without us even noticing.

Steffan swings himself over the railing and drops down to the yard beside me as Jared – still grinning – wanders on ahead. Steff drapes his arm around my shoulder and ruffles my hair affectionately with his knuckles (which he knows I hate). "Boy's alright. You'll see." Then, with a smart rap on the top of my head, he cackles and steps aside. Hands in his pockets, whistling, he strides into the sunshine after Jared.

There's a stack of oil drums beside a building on one

side of the yard. The wall next to them is stained with rust where water has been dripping from a cracked gutter and litter has collected between the drums, trapped by a mass of spider webs. But behind the building…behind the building more than makes up for it.

Sitting at the base of the hill, and marked out by the omnipresent blue railings, there is the most beautiful pool I've ever seen. It's not a swimming pool – not at all. It's a miniature lake. It's shallow and wide, and the walkway which surrounds it is overhung with lush trees whose branches tumble towards the surface of the water. Fish glint in the sunlight as they flit about. On a little concrete island in the middle, cast to look like rock, there's a gold statue looking…shiny. Above us, the sky is a perfect shade of summer blue – it's too early in the day yet for it to bleach to heatwave-white – and reflected in the water, it makes me think of the sea.

This is one of the temples.

"Woah." That's Steffan. He's stopped dead in his tracks. "Wasn't expecting that."

He's asking for it. I duly oblige. "What *were* you expecting?"

"I dunno. More sheds. Just…not that."

The three of us stand there, side by side, staring at it; this place, this temple, this unexpected, unanticipated thing. A few minutes ago, I was kicking myself for insisting we go looking for the elephant – but now I'm glad we did. I've never been in a temple before but I suppose I imagined it would be kind of the same as a church, and it's not at all. Not even close. I thought it would feel the same, all stern and reverent and sensible; weighted down by history and solemnity and purpose. But this? It's joyful.

The dents, the rust, the flaking paint...they're not pretty but they can't hide the fact that this place meant something. It still does. A few knocks can't take that away from it.

"It's still here, Jared." I don't know whether I mean to say the words aloud, but I do anyway.

"What?"

"Look. It's still here. Whatever else he did, this is still here. It's just waiting. It'll be okay."

"You're right. Back to calling him a wanker, then." He nudges me, and my heart tumbles over itself beneath my ribs.

Jared's going to be alright.

# twelve

Steffan makes himself scarce when I finally pull out my phone to call Amy back. It's like he thinks that me seeing him and my phone in the same place at the same time will cause some kind of massive temper-flashback and before he can defend himself I'll have pinned him down on the ground and be beating him about the head with a log. I consider the mental image for a moment, before accepting the sad fact that there's no way I could keep him pinned down. He weighs more than I do.

Jared, who is carrying the tents back to the car, walks past. "Stop fantasizing about maiming him, Lim. Move on…"

"Was it that obvious?"

Without breaking his stride, he shifts the weight of the tents to his shoulder, spins around so he's walking backwards and nods, before laughing and spinning back around again.

If I play my cards right, they'll have got everything back in the car by the time I'm done with Amy.

Amy answers her phone on the second ring. She's been waiting for me, hasn't she? Do I get a hello, a good morning, a how-are-you-on-this-glorious-day? No.

"Finally!"

"Look, Amy, can we just…" I rub my hand over my forehead like I'll find the right words stuck to it. (I don't.) "You're pissed, I'm sorry, can we leave it at that?"

Her voice is reproachful. "You were supposed to call me…"

"I've been trying to! The reception here's terrible. I've spent the last twenty minutes looking for a good enough signal." The lie trips gently, cheerfully, off my tongue. The fact is that I just didn't want to call. Not because of her (although that's how she'd take it if I told her the truth) but because while I'm here, I can imagine that this is any other summer. Any summer at all but this one. And that when it's over, everything will carry on just the same as it always has. At the other end of the phone, Amy either believes me or she doesn't. It doesn't really matter.

"I just want to make sure you're having a good time."

"You just want to make sure I'm staying out of trouble, you mean."

"That too. Don't hate me for it."

"I'm fine."

"You're fine? You're sure?"

"I'm sure." I pause, hold my breath, listen. I almost don't want to ask the question. "How's Dad?"

There's a sudden change in the sound coming from the other end of the phone, and I can hear birds singing; an aeroplane passing overhead. She's taken the phone out into the garden. So that's how Dad is.

"He's...okay." She considers the word very carefully. "The doctor's coming at ten."

"I thought he was coming yesterday?" I think back to the noise in her voicemail.

"No, that was someone else."

"A different doctor?"

"Something like that."

"Who exactly? If the GP's coming today..."

"Not the GP. It's a hospital doctor."

"What for?"

"It's nothing for you to panic about, okay? Your dad's just...well, you know he's struggling. Everything that's happened...your mum. It was just too much, and I'm worried about him – I know you are too. It's one of the reasons I thought you could do with a couple of days away from here while he gets himself together. While we get him some help. We'll talk—"

"I'm coming back. I'll tell Steffan I need to come home."

"You don't need—"

"I'm coming back..." I talk over her, covering her words with my own.

"I can't take care of both of you," she snaps, loud enough to stop me.

"I don't need taking care of." My voice is barely even a whisper, and at first I'm not sure she heard me. But then she sighs.

"I'm sorry. That wasn't what I meant, and I shouldn't have said it. I just...I want you to have a break, to be with your friends. To have some time."

"Steff is moving. To America."

"I know."

"Oh."

She knew. She knew that Steff was going, and she didn't tell me. And then I realize that this was why she was so fine with us doing this, why it was okay for me to just pack a bag and promise to call. So unlike it would have been with my mother. Amy knew. She wanted me to say goodbye.

More secrets. I'm so very tired of them.

Did Steff tell her himself? I wonder. Did his dad? Or did she pick it up through hearsay and gossip and whispers in the queue at the post office? Does everyone else in town already know? How long has Amy known about this? I ask myself, as I half-listen to the rest of what she has to say: things about wanting to protect me, to give me a break.

Being worried that I was finding life tough enough right now…

Nothing she says has any weight to it. It's all just words to me. Words and secrets and reasons for keeping them. Reasons like: because it's no one else's business. Because what would people think? Because someone's feelings might get hurt.

Bullshit. The lot of it. Secrets get out – they always will. It's what makes them so dangerous, so toxic. A secret is like a tumour, an infection; something lying hidden beneath the surface, but always, always spreading a web of telltale poison lines across its keeper's skin. You can cover them up, you can paint over them…but you can never really hide them.

Like with Mum. I saw – eventually. Amy saw. My father saw. We are all guilty. We are all to blame.

Steffan and Jared both saw, I know. Becca saw, as I know all too well. (And god, I hope she's got a bruise where I smacked her one. A great big puffy purple bruise. It's the least of what she deserves.) And if she saw, then everyone saw. What's the point of pretending, of keeping a secret which was never mine to keep, and which everybody already knows, however quiet we tried to keep it? To protect a dead woman? What for? She's already dead. She saw to that.

It takes a long time to drink yourself to death. To really and truly, *properly* drink yourself to death, without turning to a razor blade or a bottle of pills in a particularly low moment. It takes dedication. Years of training.

Some people train their whole lives to become athletes or astronauts.

My mother spent hers training to become an alcoholic.

# thirteen

"Functional" is a shitty word.

Computers are "functional". The bathrooms in motorway hotels are "functional"; their three-quarter-length baths anything but.

When I was nine, my mother bought me the ugliest pair of school shoes I'd ever seen, instead of the ones with the hidden key in the sole. I don't know why I wanted them so badly, but I did. They were magical. They had a *hidden thing in them*. The shoes I got were, on the other hand, dull and boring and black with a buckle.

Functional.

Shoes. Computers. Cheap hotel bathrooms.

Not people. People are not, should never be, functional.

Unless, of course, they're alcoholics. Then we say they're "functional" like it's a good thing.

The big things sneak up on you. It probably snuck up

on her. Awful as it sounds, I'd rather think of it that way: that by the time she realized what she was doing, what was happening to her – what she was – it was too late. The alternative? The alternative is that she made that choice and she stuck with it, and all those bottles that Amy just cleared out from under the sink and in the garden shed… that was the path she chose.

Drinking yourself to death isn't glamorous. It's not Dean Martin and the Rat Pack and all those golden Hollywood stars that Jared loves so much. It's jitters and night sweats and not being able to speak. It's hands that shake so badly that writing a shopping list is like writing Hamlet.

The slide is deceptively slow – slow enough not to notice if you don't know what to look for. It's like the sea eating away at a cliff. You don't know what's happening until one day the cliff crashes into the sea. When it comes – and it will – there's no time for goodbye. It's just…over. It's only when you look back, when you start finding all the clues that were left behind, that you realize you should have seen it coming. But you understand this all too late, because foresight is a luxury you just didn't have.

And here's the other thing nobody tells you about that life: it doesn't just cast a shadow before it, it leaves an echo behind. Why else is Amy throwing out a drinker's stash when the drinker is no longer here to drink it?

Why do you think?

There's only two other people who live in that house – and like I said, vodka's not my thing.

I know what kind of doctor is coming to see my father, and I know why my aunt doesn't want me there. They're hoping to save him from himself, from the slide. They're shoring up the cliff before it crumbles – or at least they're trying to.

Steffan watched his mother wither away, eaten from the inside by something she couldn't control. I watched mine give up on everything but the bottle, and when I picked up the clothes the paramedics had cut off her and I pulled the sodden sheets from the bed, I wrapped them all in plastic and I threw them in the bin.

My mother used to play patience in the winter. It was always around six o'clock in the evening, and she'd finish up whatever it was she was doing. Dinner was either cooking or was something fast enough that she didn't have to worry about it for a while, and she'd pour herself a drink and put on opera and she'd sit down and deal out the cards. It was like a ritual, I guess; I'd come down from my room and homework or whatever and I'd find her sitting at the table in the living room moving tens onto nines or shuffling kings into empty spaces while she waited for my father to come home from work.

She tried to teach me; did teach me patience (oh, the irony, yes) and racing demon. She once tried to teach me poker, but I was about ten or something and refused because, well, *Mother*, right? And now I really, really wish I knew how to play because it would actually be kind of a cool thing to be able to do.

I always thought the card games were just her way of marking time between the phases of the day: once the afternoon was over but before the evening could really begin. It never occurred to me that it wasn't a way of killing the time; that it was actually a reward for making it through another day of a life that was – for whatever reason, and who says there even was one – killing *her*. The cards weren't the ritual. The drink was.

It was a Manhattan, to begin with. Patience and a Manhattan. And then it was patience and two Manhattans. And then it was just the Manhattans, no cards.

And somewhere, sometime, it changed again. It wasn't a cocktail any more. It was wine.

Because that's better, right?

Only what nobody saw, and what we all found out too late, was that what we thought was plain old white wine was actually laced with vodka; one stashed within the other like a Russian doll, hiding in plain sight.

I don't remember when she stopped using the wine.

\* \* \*

140

Could I have saved her? That's *my* secret; the question that keeps me awake – the question which, last night, for the first night in fourteen, I forgot to ask. Could I have changed the story, switched the ending? If I had taken away a glass of wine at dinner; had diluted the vodka down to nothing under the tap? If I had said something, would it have made a difference, or would it already have been too late? Could I have done *anything*? Was it better to let her think I didn't see? Kinder, or more cruel?

Even though it's Steffan who lost his mother to a disease which carried her off with barely a backward glance, it's Jared who would understand how this feels.

All of us are scarred, but some of us are guiltier than others.

# fourteen

I've barely said goodbye to Amy when Steffan, already over by the car and *always* the master of subtlety, decides that the best way to get my attention is to hoot the horn of the Rust Bucket loudly and repeatedly – all the while yelling a load of, frankly, astonishingly filthy stuff. I can only hope Random Dude from the Vale isn't in earshot…but at the same time, I can't stop myself from smiling. Steff has never been good at real affection. Taking the piss? Sure. But honest affection – love, I guess – not so much. When his mum died, it was like he hid his heart somewhere; locked it in a box with a key like the ones in those shoes I wanted so badly, and put it away. I see flashes of it from time to time. A single heartbeat's worth maybe, but it's there.

"In the car, Limpet. In the car now, or you're walking home…" His voice carries across the lane and into the field. I walk faster towards the car.

Like he'd leave.

The sound of the car engine starting, then revving as loudly as the poor thing probably can without exploding, makes me jump. He wouldn't.

Would he?

Actually, given the chance he probably would.

I start running.


"Alright?" Steffan's sitting on the car bonnet when I get there. "Where's the fire?" His face is tilted up towards the sun, his eyes hidden behind his sunglasses. Inside the car, Jared's smirking from behind a pair of knock-off Wayfarers (like I said: so Hollywood). Although he's sitting in the passenger seat, I can see his right foot resting on the accelerator; his knee crooked awkwardly across the centre console. The engine growls as he twitches his foot and the pair of them snigger.

"Very bloody funny."

"Serves you right for leaving us to lug your bag and tent round."

"I'm sorry; were the big strong rugby boys struggling with the girly bag?" I'm unimpressed. "Did you break a fingernail?"

Slowly, Steffan tilts his head back down to face me, peering over the top of his glasses. "In the car, girly."

He slides down from the bonnet as I climb – somewhat reluctantly – into the back seat. If anything, the car's even hotter than yesterday. It feels like I'm climbing into an oven.

"Jesus, Steff. You could fry eggs in here."

"Open a window, then." Things rattle ominously as he slams his door shut.

"Ha ha ha. Such a comedian." I pull a face. He ignores it. "So what's today?"

They look at each other blankly. And then they both turn and look at me – just as blankly.

"Today? Saturday?" Steff offers.

Clueless. Utterly clueless.

I roll my eyes. I'm already sweating. The car smells of something not dissimilar to unwashed feet. Not my feet, I can tell you. It's *rank*. Whose stupid idea was this road trip, anyway?

"Beach," I say.

"Beach yourself," Steffan pings back at me. It's an old joke. A very, very old one which is clearly way past saving, like an old mug hidden under a bed.

"Are we going yet? I'm bored. And hot."

Jared opens his mouth to say something, then closes it again and shakes his head. Steffan snorts. I pick up the magazine lying on the back seat and start leafing through it. I'm not going to rise to the bait.

Finally, Steffan settles himself into his seat and fastens his belt with a click. "Fine," he says as he puts the car into gear. "Beach it is."

We've been driving for a good ten minutes before I look out of the window and realize. We're heading towards the estuary.

"Umm, Steff..." I toss the magazine aside. "You're not thinking about Llansteffan, are you?"

"Mmmppphhffwah?" Crumbs go all over the dashboard. I can see them from here. Always eating.

"It's like you live under a rock. The diesel, remember?"

There's another shower of crumbs and a growl, but he swings the car into a U-turn on the deserted road. It's barely wide enough, and there's a clatter of brambles and branches along the side of the car as we scrape the hedge, but it's fine.

He'd forgotten about the diesel.

It was a couple of weeks ago now, and it wasn't much, but it was all anyone could talk about for a while. A bunch of townies "acquired" a few barrels of red diesel and were trying to sell them – but when a particularly interested member of our local police force stopped their van and asked them a couple of questions, they panicked and dumped the whole lot into the stream above Llansteffan.

They poisoned the stream, the fish, the plants and – because the stream feeds down across the beach to the estuary – the sand. Nice going, boyos.

"Right, then. Change of plan. We'll…er…?" Steffan drums his fingers on the steering wheel.

Jared doesn't look away from his window. "The Havens."

Steff glances up into the rear-view, waits for me to nod or shake my head. My mother grew up in the Havens. It's where she used to spend her summers; summers just like this one, with friends just like these. To sit on the beach there, now, will be like dancing with her barefoot on the sand.

I nod.

"Alright, then. The Havens." Steffan flicks the indicator on and takes the next turning off the road onto an even narrower one.

I recognize the way Steffan looks at me in the mirror. After all, I've seen it enough recently. When someone you love dies on you – a mother, a father, whoever – it's like you're helpless. Powerless. Watching your friend go through that is a kind of helplessness too.

I can see it clearly in Steffan's face. He doesn't say it, doesn't speak the words aloud. He doesn't need to; I can read him well enough to know. He's watching for splinters, watching for signs. He's doing his best to light my way so that I don't lose myself in the shadows. It never occurs to him that perhaps I don't want to be found. Not yet. I don't want someone to light my way: I want to find it for myself. And when I've had enough of being in the dark, I'll open the blinds or light a candle or do whatever it is that we do when we're ready to stop hiding. I don't want the pity or the sympathy or the nervous glances back in the mirror. Not from him. Especially not from him. Did I look at him like that, when it was his turn? I suppose I did. I must have. And is this how it goes – that we each have our "turn" at this? Steff first, now me...and someday, Jared too. Will he look at us and find the two of us looking back at him like that when it's his turn?

And then I remember. No. He won't. Steffan will be on the other side of the world. Between everything else, I'd forgotten about that. How could I forget? Steffan is leaving...no, not leaving. Being *taken*.

Sitting in the back of the car, I feel like an invisible hand has slipped around my throat and tightened, cutting off my air. Steffan will be gone in no time. My best friend, gone. Just like that. Another thing I'm powerless to change, another thing that I have to stand back and accept. Helpless.

I don't want to be helpless. I'm not some damsel in distress, walled into a tower and waiting for a knight to swing by and rescue me. I don't *do* helpless.

I can't see Jared in the rear-view. All I can see is the back of his head in front of me. It's not giving me any answers – but at least he can't be giving me That Look from the back of his head. And that's the thing: Jared looks at me differently from Steffan. He always has, hasn't he? I'd never thought about it before now – I've never needed to – but he's always seemed more distant. Cooler. After all, Steffan is Steffan and Jared is Jared and never the two are alike.

My mind fills with the memory of Jared, leaning against the tree in the graveyard. Jared, standing guard outside the changing block; peeling off his T-shirt in the sunshine; standing in what's left of Barley Vale.

My head is full of Jared and my heart pounds and as Steffan misses a turn, swears and hurls the car into a three-point turn, I can't tell whether it's the movement or the memories making my stomach lurch.

As we bump along, I cling on to the door. "So, when're you getting those driving lessons, Steff?"

"Driving lessons, you say...?"

Uh-oh.

Steffan takes the junction he'd missed, then almost immediately turns again – this time onto a road that's little more than a bunch of potholes strung together with gravel. Definitely uh-oh.

"Private road," he says, pulling over and releasing his seat belt. The ignition's still running as he jiggles the gear stick into neutral and yanks up the handbrake so hard the suspension creaks.

Very uh-oh.

Steffan turns to look at me. "Out," he says, and he can barely hide his own amusement.

Oh, god. I know exactly what he's thinking. He's been threatening this for a while.

"No way."

"Yes way."

"Don't have a licence."

"Don't need one." He wags a finger at the sign saying *Private road*, right beside us. Just to clarify.

"Steff…"

"Oh, come on. Stop being such a baby. You'll have to learn sometime, won't you?"

I shoot a quick glance at Jared in the vague hope he might come to my rescue. The look on his face tells me in no uncertain terms that gallantry is dead and I Am On My Own with this one.

"*Fine.*" I manage to tangle myself up in all the crap around me and mostly fall out of the back seat. Steffan holds the driver's door open. No escape.

"Your chariot, my lady."

"Piss off. And don't think I'll forget this in a hurry."

"Your memory is indeed long, my lady."

"Five minutes."

Jared has unfolded himself from the passenger seat and is leaning against a post outside, giving his space up to Steffan. If his grin was any wider, the bottom half of his jaw would drop off. I peer out of the car at him. "And you. Don't think I haven't noticed you. You're enjoying this far too much."

"You bet I am." He folds his arms and winks at me, and my hands tighten around the steering wheel of their own accord.

I can feel the car vibrating under my feet. Well. I say "vibrating". It's more like rattling. It wasn't exactly in the best shape when Steffan bought it, and having had to put up with his abuse, it's just about on its last legs. Or wheels. As if to prove its point, the engine coughs, stutters and makes a peculiar chugging sound. Outside the car, one of Jared's eyebrows shoots up.

"You might want to get that looked at," he says.

Steffan makes a snorting noise and waves a hand at him. "What for? You think I can take it with me?"

Of course. Tick-tock tick-tock, time's a-wastin'.

He's saying things about pedals and camber and the gear stick and *something*, and frankly I haven't a clue. There's something about one of the stalks sticking out of the steering console. I'm supposed to push it up. I do. The windscreen wipers swish back and forth across the glass.

"Not *that* one."

"Sorry." I try to push it back down again. A jet of water shoots out of the bottom of the windscreen, arching up and sideways and spraying Jared (who by now is leaning on the

150

roof of the car, peering in through the still-open passenger door – if I didn't know better, I'd think Steffan had left it open in case he needed to bail out in a hurry...). Jared splutters and then dissolves into howls of laughter.

"Piss *off*. I mean it."

He's too busy laughing to answer.

Steffan's still wittering on about something to do with gears and pound coins and setting a clutch... All I'm getting is: *You're in charge of a ton of metal with about a million moving parts and your best mate is in the seat next to you and you're probably going to kill everyone, but hey, everybody dies anyway, right?*

I doubt that's what he's actually saying.

Eventually, he sighs. "Give me your hand, would you?"

"Uh-uh. Not that kind of girl."

"Dream on." He leans over, grabbing my hand and planting it firmly on the top of the gear stick. The list of things I have to do all at the same time is right up there with tap-dancing while patting my head and rubbing my stomach and counting backwards from 397 (in German) – but suddenly, and without me quite understanding how or why, we're creeping forward...

And then, with an almighty great lurch, we're not.

"Stalled it," mutters Steffan.

"Yay?"

"No. Not yay."

The laughter outside the car has progressed to full-blown hysterics. There are actual tears running down Jared's face, and he's no longer leaning against that post: he's clinging on to it so he doesn't fall over.

It's nice to have friends, isn't it?

After what feels like an eternity of more backwards-counting Germanic tap-dancing, the engine splutters into life and the Rust Bucket inches forward. I'm driving. I am the captain of the good ship We're Going To Die Horribly In This Metal Box And Oh God What Do I Do Now?

"See? Not so bad, is it?"

"Can't talk. Trying not to kill us." My fingers are wrapped so tightly around the steering wheel that my fingernails are turning white. If I loosen my grip even slightly, that's it. Game over. Steff slouches back into his seat. Well, I'm glad one of us is relaxed. You know, while I'm busy sweating into the wheel.

"Uh, Steff?"

"Mmm?" The bastard's actually wedged his knees against the glovebox and has closed his eyes.

"There's, like, a thing."

"A thing?"

"A thing. You know. A...*thing.*" My brain can only handle so much at a time. The car stuff is taking up so much processing power that I have apparently lost the power of normal speech.

"Go round it, then."

"How?" I grip the wheel even tighter.

It's a gatepost. A metal gatepost.

Wait. There are two of them.

(How is this a surprise? Of *course* there are two of them. They're *either side of a gate*.)

Ahead, the almost-road begins to narrow. The low wire-and-post fencing running either side of it angles in, ending at a wide galvanized metal gate. Which is open. Beyond it, the road disappears altogether and turns into a large, lumpy field.

I make an unhappy squeaking sound. Reluctantly, Steffan opens an eye. "Just keep going straight on and through the gate."

"But…"

"It's fine. You could fit at least two of this car through there, okay?"

"It's just…"

"Why are you going right?" Both of his eyes are open.

"I'm not."

"You are!" He sits up.

"You said go straight on…"

"Stop looking at me and *look where you're going!*"

We have swung wildly to the right and I'm now steering us straight at the right gatepost and the edge of the metal gate. I do what I do best when I'm panicked. I freeze.

We're still inching forward. The needle on the speedometer is barely off the pin…and yet the gatepost looms ahead of us; suddenly it's as large and unavoidable as a cliff face. And there is nothing I can do…

"Seriously, Lim. Brake?"

"Can't."

"The pedal, Lim. Brake."

"Oh." I glance down at my feet. He sees one of my knees twitch.

"Not that one – the other one."

"Which one?"

"The *other* one!"

The gatepost is still there. Still getting bigger.

I stamp both my feet on the floor of the car, pressing down all three pedals at once. There's an awful sound from the engine, and Steffan's resorted to shouting at me in Welsh – much bloody good might it do him – and he's yanking the wheel to the left and hauling up the handbrake and with a final howl and a cough from the engine, we've stopped.

My heart is pounding in my throat and my hands are slick with sweat. Suddenly, there's a voice in my right ear. "The only thing you could crash into for a mile, and you head right for it…"

I scream, the rush of adrenaline breaking my trance as Jared jumps away from the window, still laughing. I disentangle myself from the seat belt and from the pedals and (after an awkward moment where I forget how to open a car door) get out of the car as fast as I can.

I'm shaking.

So's Jared – but in his case it's with laughter. There are creases around his eyes that I don't think I've ever seen before. They make him look both younger and older at the same time, and in amongst the panic and the embarrassment and the everything else, I wonder what he was like as a kid. Before.

"Thank you for your concern, Jared." I don't sound quite as offended as I'd like to – and his laughter's infectious, even if it's entirely at my own expense.

Steffan slams the car door. "Well. *My* life just flashed before my eyes."

"I told you it was a bad idea."

"Promise me something, would you?"

"What?" I fold forwards, resting my hands on my knees.

"That you'll wait till I'm in another country before you try driving again?"

His scowl breaks into a smile. Jared's still giggling and I can't help myself any longer – and then all three of us are there, standing around a little lane in the middle of the countryside, laughing because suddenly there's no reason not to.

# fifteen

"I'm telling you – it's him."

"It's never. Seriously. No way."

We are in the supermarket. The glamour. But having survived a night in the wild and my traumatic first driving lesson earlier, I have demanded my reward.

No, obviously it's not a trip to the local supermarket.

I want a picnic on the beach, seeing as that's where we're meant to be going. You have to have a picnic on the beach on a summer road trip, don't you? It's the *law*. And, with only a few days to fit in "all the usual places", it has to happen today. Because I say so. An actual picnic, involving something a little more exciting than the two or three packets of crisps which have survived Steffan and Jared's locust-attacks and the half bottle of flat lemonade that's been rolling around inside the spare wheel in the boot and the two bottles of warm beer which have kept wedging themselves under my lower back. Not to mention those bloody cigars Steffan's nicked from his dad, which I'm sure will make an appearance at some point. I'm kind of hoping he's forgotten about them; what with Jared's sly little cigarette habit, if Steff starts puffing away on a bunch of cigars, I'm going to have to do something really outrageous just to keep up. No idea what, of course, but I'm sure I could come up with something if I really put my mind to it.

Jared has gone to raid the deli counter for cooked chicken, leaving Steffan and me to hunter-gather everything else. And that's when we spot the most loathed of all our teachers picking over the fruit and veg. Being the mature types we are, we both immediately turn tail and hide behind the milk fridge, peering round to spy on him. It's obvious he hears something, as he glances up from the aubergine he's busy feeling up, but we're saved by the racks of semi-skimmed.

When you're a kid, you kind of believe that your teachers live in school; that somewhere in the staffroom there's a little row of beds and, come seven thirty in the evening, they all tuck themselves up with their hot-water bottles and a cup of tea and go to sleep. Of course, you soon realize that teachers have lives outside of school (and that some of them – shocker – even have *families*) but there's still something so weird about seeing them outside school boundaries. Wearing…shorts. Buying *vegetables*.

Mr Lewis is the teacher I would have least expected to see out in the wild. In fact, up until this very moment, I was still absolutely convinced someone just folded him up and put him in a desk drawer at the end of the day, and then shook him out and dusted him down again the next morning. He's tried to fail me at physics twice in the past year. I'm starting to take it personally.

I don't even know why we're hiding.

It just seemed like the thing to do.

I mean, it's not like he can give us detention for having a basket that's filled mainly with sausage rolls, is it? What's he going to do – call our mothers?

Yeah. Good luck with that.

"What are you *doing*?"

Jared has appeared behind us, clutching not one, not two...but *three* bags of cooked chicken. There are shiny grease spots soaking through the waxy paper in several places. It makes me feel vaguely sick.

"It's Loopy Lewis," says Steffan, jerking his head towards the vegetable stands.

"And you're hiding...why?" He drops the chicken into the shopping basket and shakes his head.

"Oh, like you'd understand," Steffan scoffs. "Mr Top-of-the-Class. Mr Suck-up. Mr—"

"Alright, point taken." Jared peers around the milk fridge. "What's he doing?"

"I don't know. Performing an experimental jazz piece?" Steff pulls a face.

"You should go into comedy, mate. You're clearly better at it than you are at physics." Jared shakes his head and wanders back up the aisle. Steffan scoops up the basket and follows him, muttering something about spicy salsa. He's not much better at physics than I am.

I peer back around the fridge. "Loopy" Lewis, as he's known, is still there, but the longer I look at him, the less I see the stroppy old teacher who's made my Thursday afternoons a misery for the last two years and the more I see...something else.

Beyond the school walls, he has none of his usual power. He's not on the platform at the front of the classroom here, or prowling up and down the spaces between the desks ready to snatch your work out from under your hand to "examine your workings" (and, in my case, usually to criticize my handwriting). He's a lonely old man, shopping for food for one. He looks sad.

I step out from behind the fridge – and, despite everything I just thought, I find myself straightening my T-shirt as I cross the aisle to the vegetable stand.

"Mr Lewis..." I tail off. I'm not quite sure what to say next. I just feel like I have to say *something*. At the top of the aisle, Steffan's head pops around the shelves. He's mouthing something at me. I blow him a kiss, and snap my hand back down just as Mr Lewis turns to look at me.

"Miss Jenkins." He's peering over the top of his glasses at me. Maybe that whole thing about him having no power over me outside school...maybe that was a mistake. He looks me up and down. "I didn't think you lived..."

"I don't. I'm just passing through. With friends."

"Friends. I see." He makes the word sound unfamiliar. Maybe it is. "I see," he says again. His eyes flicker across the surrounding shelves.

His fingers, wrapped around the wire handle of the shopping basket he's carrying, look so much thinner now than they do when they're pointing out the mistakes in equations. They're bone wrapped in thin skin, speckled with scars and long-faded freckles. And that's as if the basket he's carrying wasn't sad enough already: one onion, a half-loaf of sliced bread, a pint of milk, three apples, two chicken breasts...

We always took the piss out of Loopy Lewis because we couldn't imagine him having a life outside school. Now I can see he really doesn't, it's not funny any more. It's sad. It's so, so sad. He's just a lonely man, trying his best to get a bunch of kids who don't really want to be there to pay attention and get them through their exams as best as he can...and then he has to do the same thing the next year, and the next, and the next.

"I just saw you, and I thought I'd say hi." My voice

sounds weak, even to me. I smile anyway. I mean it, which surprises me.

"Well, that's very nice of you," he says in a tone I've never heard him use before. It's a non-teacher voice... something your neighbour would use when you've dropped off a parcel you took in for them. Not at all what I've come to expect from him. He pushes his glasses up his nose.

"I was sorry to hear about your mother..." He lowers his voice, and there it is. The pity stare.

Mr Lewis is giving *me* the pity stare.

"Thanks."

And just like that, Funeral Limpet is back: the one who nods and is sensible and sombre and makes tea for police officers when they're standing on the upstairs landing and tries to help the funeral director sort out the flowers. She would never climb out of a car sunroof just because it was too hot inside. She would never try and drive her best friend's car. She would never wonder what the skin just above Jared's collarbone would smell like, up close...of smoke, or sweat, or sunshine...

Mr Lewis is saying something to me, only his words are coming out all wrong. Or maybe I'm hearing them all wrong – and he's suddenly narrowing his eyes at me and there's a hot flush creeping up my face from my chin to my eyebrows and is it warm in here all of a sudden or is it just me?

161

I pull myself together and his voice fades back in. He's trying to be kind – he's saying all the things you say to a kid whose mother just died and who the whole town's whispering about. And then, I realize, he actually means them. All the things he's saying, all the words – he *means* them.

He's one of the only people who has, and I can barely stop myself from hugging him.

I admit, this is not how I saw this going.

He looks over my shoulder, past me, to the end of the aisle. The smallest of smiles flickers across his features. "It would appear that the other Musketeers are waiting for you."

Wait. What?

That's not possible. It's just not. The Three Musketeers joke is a private one; one which has never even been outside my head, let alone been handed in to my physics teacher (who is probably the closest thing to a nemesis I'm ever going to get – would that make him Rochefort or the Cardinal…?).

He sees my shock. I think he probably enjoys it, because he chuckles and peers over his glasses one more time and says, "You aren't the only one looking out at the world, you know. And you certainly aren't the only one who notices what book someone is carrying when they walk into a classroom. Particularly not when it's as well-read as your copy."

And quite suddenly, he pats my arm – hesitant, but friendly – then he wanders off, leaving me staring after him and wondering whether my physics teacher is, in fact, psychic.

# *sixteen*

I've never liked the feel of sand in between my toes. Maybe it's because, when I was little, most of the time said sand was estuary sand from Llansteffan or Pembrey. Muddy and damp, it clots between your toes and clings to them and refuses to come off. I've always wondered what it must be like to walk along one of those tropical beaches where the sand is as white as bone; fine enough to flow like water if you scoop it up into the palm of your hand and let it fall. And where there are coconut trees. I don't even like coconuts, but they feel like they're an integral part of the picture, so…

We aren't likely to find many beaches matching that description around here and especially given the time we have is only *"A couple of nights, maybe…"* But this beach, this *particular* beach, is a good enough substitute. Well. It's a beach and the sand's not too muddy. So I'll make an exception and take off my shoes as soon as we're off the concrete slipway and onto the sand. Behind us, there are a couple of pubs, a tiny post office and the smallest souvenir shop you've ever seen – all of which are doing a roaring trade in (respectively) cold beer, postcards with dolphins on and inflatable dolphins. The pub nearest to the ramp is called – no prizes for guessing – The Dolphin.

Yes. This is where you come if you like dolphins. To my left you'll note the board advertising the "dolphin watching" boat trips into the bay. To my right? The bay. Featuring a complete and total lack of dolphins.

I know.

Luckily, I can take or leave the dolphins.

"I hate sand," says Steffan. He's already managed to stick his foot into some kind of mini-dune, so his shoe's full of it. He kicks his lower leg out with every step, trying to shake it all out – but the only thing he seems to be doing is making himself look like an idiot.

Even more so than usual.

Of course, Jared's trailing behind, and I know even without checking exactly how he looks. Because it's how he always looks. Movie-star Jared, weighed down by the consequences of someone else's actions. If his dad hadn't gone to prison, hadn't mucked everything up, would Jared be different? Would he be like Simon and Rhodri and all the other boyos round here who think they're something special? Or would he still be…Jared? Would he still be the one who hangs back, who keeps quiet until he has something to say? Is it the weight that makes him who he is, who he will be? Is he his father's son in that, at least?

And if he is – if he was shaped by his father's actions – what does that mean for me? What am I? What will I be, years down the line?

"Are we there yet?" Bloody Steffan.

"Oh, come on. At least let's get round the cliff into the bay…"

"What for? It's still all just sand, isn't it?"

"I get it. You're not a fan."

Part of it is him sulking because he's had to leave the violin in the car. Even he's not daft enough to bring it out here – but he's paranoid that someone'll steal the Rust Bucket and take his baby with it. I've pointed out that there is no reason, godly or ungodly, why *anyone* in their right minds would want to steal that car, but he's still not happy. He wants to sit where he can see the parking bay by the sea wall where we've left it (although how he thinks this will make any difference at all, other than his potentially being able to wave goodbye to his car and his beloved violin – not to mention my phone, which is buried somewhere under all the crap in the back – as they drive off up the hill, I don't know…).

He can sit there if he wants. I want to be around the cliff,

166

in the bay, where there's nothing but the rocks behind me, the sea before me, the sand below me and the sky above me.

And these two. Obviously.

Mostly because between them, they're carrying my picnic…

"Here," I say.

Steffan immediately drops the carrier bags he's holding. "About bloody time. You know if the tide comes in, we're screwed?"

"Tide, schmide." I have one of the sleeping bags tucked under my arm. Of course it's not mine – I'm not that daft. It's Steffan's. He just doesn't realize that. The sea's about as far out as it could possibly be – not only do we have hours before it comes anywhere near cutting us off in the bay, we'll see it coming in plenty of time. It's not like we're pitching camp, is it? I shake out the sleeping bag and plonk myself down on top of it before Steffan (who's now eyeing it suspiciously) has a chance to object.

Jared sets his bags down a little more carefully than Steffan and looks around. He's measuring the place, weighing it as though this is the first time he's ever been here. The sun catches his hair, turning it through shades of russet and gold as he moves his head this way and that, looking first up at the cliffs and the rocks behind us and then back out to sea.

"You've been here before, right?" I ask. After all, it was *his* suggestion, wasn't it?

He shrugs. "Not for a long time. Not since I was a kid." He looks like he's about to say something else, but there's a rustling sound and his face suddenly lights up. Steffan's found the sausage rolls. The pair of them are lost to me, instantly.

It's funny, because although Jared perked up the moment he realized food was happening, I'm sure that what I saw just before – just for a second – was a flash of the real him. Not the front, not the mask he puts on for everyone, including us. I saw *Jared* under there.

"You're thinking," says Steffan between mouthfuls, peering at Jared. There are pastry crumbs *everywhere*. And not a sausage roll to be seen. A whole variety of snack foods are in serious danger of becoming extinct before my very eyes. And before I have a chance to eat any of them.

For two blokes who really weren't keen on the idea of a picnic, they're not holding back when it comes to the eating part.

"Just remembering," says Jared. "Once, when I was about seven, I climbed that. It looks smaller than it used to." He nods towards the face of the cliff a little way behind us. There are chunks of rock sticking out of it at crazy angles, leading to some kind of shelf halfway up. I can see it reflected in his sunglasses when he turns his head towards me.

"Steff, you've eaten all the sausage rolls. You pig!" I turn over the empty packet for emphasis. Steffan shrugs.

"I regret nothing." He's already moved on to a packet of breadsticks. And when I say "moved on to", I mean he's using two of them as drumsticks, hitting the top of a pot of dip.

Jared stands and lopes around the edge of the makeshift picnic blanket towards me, dropping into a crouch by my side. I can feel the heat from his arms on mine, he's that close. I can almost – *almost* – feel the hairs on my forearms rising.

"The last survivor," he says, holding out his hand.

It's a sausage roll.

The last sausage roll.

I look at it. Then at him.

"You think I can't fend for myself, is that it? Pity food. You're offering me pity food."

"Pity food's still food. You should take me up on it."

"Pity. Food."

"Do you know what I had to risk to get this before he did? Do you know the deep personal sacrifice *I'm* making here?"

"It's a sausage roll, Jared."

"No. This is not *a* sausage roll. This is the *last* sausage roll."

Steffan ends it. "For god's sake…" he says and, leaning forward, he grabs the sausage roll in question and shoves it in his mouth.

I stare at him. And then I reach down and grab the first thing I can get my hands on (which happens to be a packet of peanuts) and lob it straight at him. For once, my aim's good and it smacks him right on his nose – and he hurls himself backwards dramatically.

"Oh, come on. That didn't hurt." I'm not sure whether I'm annoyed or not.

Steffan's still flat on his back, and he's still chewing that bloody pastry, but he answers anyway. "Course not. I'm just shocked you actually managed to hit me."

Is it wrong to hate your best friend just a little?


They have, predictably, brought a rugby ball with them. I have no idea where they stashed it, because if I'd seen it I would have scowled disapprovingly at it. Our deal was "picnic", not "pelting up and down the beach showing off". But Steffan is Steffan and Jared is Jared and you put the two of them in a wide open space for long enough and that's what they'll do.

I don't get it. They're basically just throwing stuff at each other. If they asked me, I'd gladly do that for them.

They wouldn't even have to go to the effort of trying to *catch* it…

I'm reasonably sure that at this distance, and from behind my sunglasses, they can't see what I'm looking at.

Or, you know, *who*.

Because suddenly he's like gravity. Something has happened and up is down and inside is outside and I'm relying on him to pull me in. It's not Steffan – Steffan who's been here before and knows the way and so desperately wants to help me. It's Jared, who is just as lost as I am, I suppose.

And maybe that's the thing. Maybe it's *because* Steffan has been through this… I can't help comparing myself to him – did he do this? Did he feel this? Is this right or wrong? How long did it take him to feel like he was himself again…?

He would never tell me how or what I should feel, I know – and I almost feel guilty for thinking it. But I do. I am. I can't stop myself comparing the way I feel to how he must have felt – just like I can't stop comparing the ways our mothers died.

The simple, awful truth of it is that I don't know whether I have the same right to grieve that Steffan did. Do I, when the ways we lost them were so very different?

Steffan has made his peace with it, I think. What happened happened. It was as impossible to know it was coming as it is to predict the path of a shooting star. It was a meteor that blazed through his skies and then, just as suddenly as it had appeared, went dark.

For me, it was like a tidal wave. A hurricane which breached every defence, every wall, every levee I could have built against it. It came from somewhere I thought I knew. The sea around me, something I never gave a second glance, suddenly turned fierce and I didn't see the wall of water coming for me until it was crashing around me, washing away the things I knew and turning the bedrock I stood on into nothing more substantial than sand.

Down the beach, Steffan whoops and throws his hands into the air, running around in a small but triumphant circle. Jared has jumped for the ball, missed and landed on his back in a cloud of sand. He's not moving. Which means he's sulking. Only a little, but you don't get to be captain of the rugby team without a hefty dose of pride, do you?

I watch as he rolls over and straightens up, dusting himself down and leaning forward to brush the sand out of his hair. I can hear Steffan chanting "Oh yeah, oh yeah, oh yeah," as he does his little victory dance, and Jared rests his hands on his knees, glancing up at me. He doesn't move, other than to flash me a grin.

A little way further back, Steffan has put one hand on his hip and appears to be doing the dance to "Greased Lightning". So when Jared explodes up from his defeated pose and bolts across the beach, sand scattering up and away behind him, Steff is caught completely off guard. I see him freeze, and I think I see him mouth the word "Shit" as he shifts his weight and starts running in the other direction.

He's fast – but he's not fast enough, and Jared has a head start. Steff puts up a good fight, ducking and dodging across the beach – but it's inevitable. He sees it coming and stops dead, throwing out his arms and tipping his head back just as Jared charges at him, tackling him and throwing him bodily to the ground.

The ball's just sitting there. It's exactly where it landed, just behind Jared's original sandy heap of shame. Which means it's not far in front of me. The two of them are still picking themselves up (predictably, Jared's bounced straight back up; Steffan's a little slower, but he's making up for it by hurling handfuls of sand at Jared, so there's that...).

I wonder.

I stretch. I stand up. I stretch some more. And then I start running, straight for the ball.

And the second I'm committed to running for it...that's when they spot me.

"Shit."

Suddenly I know how Steffan felt.

Only I've got *both* of them running full-tilt at me.

"Shitshitshitshitshit…" I run faster, but the sand is softer here and it sucks at my heels, slowing me down.

I throw a single, desperate glance around me…and there they are. They're flanking me. *Oh god…*

True to form, I stop exactly where I am and throw my hands around my head, screwing my eyes shut. I'm fully expecting to be sacked, tackled, whatever you want to call it…but instead, I find myself being lifted off my feet and scooped up. Steffan. Steffan has reached me first.

And he's not putting me down.

In fact, he's jogging towards the water.

He's still jogging towards the water.

"Don't. You. Dare."

"Never had you down as a rugby fan, Lim." He's wading into the water.

"Steffan, I swear…"

"I always figured swimming was much more your thing."

"*Steffan…!*"

The arms that are supporting me suddenly whip away, and I'm flying through the air before I have a chance to yell…and I hit the water with a splash.

# seventeen

Because they are bastards, the pair of them are standing there at the edge of the waves, taking photos of me on their phones – which of *course* they brought down with them from the car. I, meanwhile, find myself sitting in shallow water, fully clothed and with my hair dripping over my face. And a mouth full of seawater.

Well, *fine*.

Dignity, Limpet. Dignity.

I smooth my hair back from my face and wipe the seawater away from my eyes. My lips taste of salt and sunscreen.

I'm not going to let them off that lightly.

The two of them are still standing around being smug and amused and, well, *them*. Fine. Fine, fine, fine.

I half-stand. I slump down again.

I half-stand again. And I slump back down.

They've stopped sniggering. Jared nudges Steffan. I can see their heads leaning closer together.

Good.

For extra effect, I rub one of my ankles.

Well. It would have been effective if a larger wave hadn't smacked into the back of me the second I leaned forward to do it.

Still.

They're coming. Jared first; Steffan a couple of steps behind him. Steffan thinks I'm trying to trick them – which, of course, I am. He knows me too well.

"Limpet?" Jared pushes his sunglasses up onto his head, squinting as sunlight hits the water.

"It's my ankle," I say. "Can you give me a hand up?"

I see him hesitate – and I can hear Steffan's hissed warning. Jared gives me a measured, sideways look and, for a second, I wonder whether he's going to dart back out of reach along with Steffan. But then he holds out his hand and I take it.

And with all my strength, I pull.

He's off-balance and topples over with surprising ease, landing almost on top of me. I can hear Steffan splashing away to safety, laughing and shouting, "I told you!"

Jared spits out a mouthful of water. He's just as wet as I am. I was hoping for Steffan, but I'll take what I can get.

"Feel better now?" he asks.

"A bit. Mostly I just feel…well, kind of soggy."

"You want to get him?"

"Yes. Yes, I do."

"You grab his feet." There's that grin of his again, and suddenly we are conspirators. "Wait till I say."

He pushes himself up and out of the water, and he holds his hand out to me. I take it, feeling his fingers close around mine for the second time. They feel strong, I notice now, but somehow rougher than they should. Rougher than I was expecting.

He wades out of the water, shaking it out of his hair and letting it drip off his fingertips. Caught in the sunlight, it looks like he leaves diamonds in his wake. Steffan's watching with his arms folded and a generally amused expression. That evaporates when Jared clamps his arms around Steff's upper body and yells "Now!" at me. I splash towards them and – as instructed – grab Steffan's feet. We have him.

"My bloody phone's in my pocket—" he begins – but he doesn't have time to finish because…whoops…he's in the water too.

Steff shakes his head rapidly, flicking water everywhere and blinks up at me. "Well, fine." He staggers to his feet, unsteady on the shifting sand – and then he winks at Jared and the two of them lunge at me – and I'm in the water again, spluttering it out under a silken sky.

177

\* \* \*

Steffan isn't happy about being wet. Not even a little. So he stomps, squelches and grumbles his way off towards the car in search of dry clothes and returns triumphant. The sun's hot enough that mine feel half-dry already, just from sitting out in it, and I don't plan on moving any time soon. Mind you, I don't say no to the towel he throws at me – and I don't say no to the beer he brings back with him either.

Following the sun, we've shifted back towards the rocks – and I've compromised with Steffan by moving a little closer to the car. Well, I say "compromised". I guess I mean that on his way back (with said beer and towel), Steff sat down at a point midway between us and the slipway and refused to move.

Jared simply shrugged. "I think he wins, doesn't he?"

"He always wins," I grumble.

Not that it's so bad. If you discount the awful smell of cigars. Because, yes, Steffan also came back with that box he lifted from his dad, and is alternately coughing and puffing away on one.

Here's the thing. I understand cigarettes. Sort of. I mean, I'm not a fan, exactly, but I get it. Cigars, though – what's that about? It's some kind of blokey posturing, isn't it? It's like when Steffan decided to get his ear pierced last year, then actually saw someone else getting theirs done and flat-out fainted in the middle of the shop. Bless him.

Steffan's prone to attacks of blokey posturing. He's the one who got so face-meltingly drunk at a party one time that we had to carry him home. He's the one who got a tooth knocked out in Newcastle Emlyn one Saturday night. He's the one who got detention for a week for bringing… well, let's not go there, shall we? And to think he has the nerve to go on about "the femrage".

Jared lies back on the sand, his T-shirt drying off on the rocks behind us. I can't see his eyes behind his sunglasses, and I don't dare look too hard in case he's watching me. One part of me wonders why on earth he'd be watching *me*, and yet part of me knows that Jared is always watching. Always. He watches everything, everybody, the way a stray cat watches the world around it from beneath a bush; hiding until it knows who to trust and who to fear.

There are few people he trusts, I know that. Steffan, of course. Me, I suppose. His grandparents. His uncle, who left last year… But who else? Not his father, that's for sure. And as for his mother…

Maybe what's happened to him is worse than either my situation or Steffan's. Our mothers are dead. One taken by cancer, one by drink. But Jared's? Jared's mother is still walking and talking and out on the town and being felt up by her new boyfriend in a taxi outside The Farmer's Arms. And even so, she's as dead to him as ours are to us – more so, maybe, because we still have their ghosts to cling to. My mother flits through my dreams, as heavy as gossamer and as dark as the moon. I feel her there, although she's gone when I wake. And I know – I *know* – that there are no real ghosts, that when we die we die and that's all there is to it. I know that all that remains of my mother is faded photographs and bones in a box and memories that already feel half-forgotten; foxed at the edges. The ghost that walks with me is of my own making: cut and stitched of my own grief and guilt. But Jared's? Jared's mother *haunts* him. Whether he's awake or asleep makes no difference.

"My god, Steff. You're going to stink." I waft my hand back and forth in front of my face in an attempt to disperse his vile little smoke cloud.

"You're saying he doesn't already?"

I'd been starting to hope that Jared was asleep. Despite my resolution not to look, I've no idea whether I've been staring at him. I mean…maybe? I don't really know. But he probably has got his eyes shut behind his shades anyway. Hopefully. He stops, his lips still parted as though he's going to say something else.

What, I wonder, would his lips taste like? Like mine, which taste of salt still? Of smoke? Not like Steffan's ridiculous cigar (which is starting to make him look a little green) but a different kind – the kind that hangs in the air and makes you think of autumn.

Jared would taste of safety, I think.

A gust of wind whips my hair into my eyes and I turn my head to brush it away...and Steffan is watching me curiously. Cigar in one hand and beer in the other, his head is cocked to one side – and it dawns on me that he has been watching me watching Jared.

Something flickers across his face; something unreadable...and then it's gone and Steffan is himself again and he's stubbing out the cigar in the sand. "Think I might go for a walk," he says queasily.

"Awesome! Me too!" I say – a little too brightly, and I know it.

Jared makes an indistinct mumbling sound and yawns, stretching his arms up and then folding them behind his head. "I'll guard the...yeah."

"Tart," says Steffan, shaking his head.

"Wanker," Jared shoots back automatically.

Steffan grins wickedly. "Is it, now? At least I—"

"Enough!" I can't bear to let him finish that sentence. I *do* have limits. He mutters something in Welsh, and Jared flicks up his middle finger as Steff rocks his beer bottle down into the sand, making a small hole to keep it upright. All I make out is "boyo" at the end, but Jared obviously hears it clearly enough because the corners of his mouth twitch into a small smile.

"You're not planning on chucking me into the sea again,

are you?" I ask as Steffan falls into step beside me, his hands deep in his pockets as he stares out at the waves.

"Dunno. Could ask you the same thing."

"You deserved it."

"So did you."

There's nothing now but the sound of the waves and the occasional seagull wheeling overhead. The tide is turning, and the swell of the current is throwing the spray higher into the air. You can smell it. We're right on the edge of the water now, but in an hour's time the spot where we stand will be under the sea. If we were to stay here, to hold fast and stand our ground, we would drown.

"You want to talk about it?" Steffan asks.

"No...and yes." I know what it is he's asking. "I just...I want it to not be my thing, you know? I don't want to be just the kid whose mother died. I mean...I guess I am already, right?' The words tumble out and alone with Steffan, I am powerless to stop them. "I just don't want to be that now, here. I don't want to be that with you guys."

There's the smallest tic at the side of his lips, but he hides it well.

"Nobody wants to be that kid, Lim. Trust me."

"I know – and that's not what I meant. I..."

"You meant that you don't want to talk about it because

talking about it makes it your…'thing'. I get it."

"I know you do."

"I'm just saying – maybe talking about it'll help."

"You never needed to…"

"You reckon?" He turns and looks me in the eyes. His gaze searches my face, sweeping over me. "You know Dad sent me to a counsellor, right?"

"No!" I'm so startled by this that it comes out as a squeak. When shocked, I sound like a hamster, apparently. *That* can be my thing.

"Oh, yeah. Every Friday after school for three months." He bends down, picks up a small, flat stone and skims it out over the water. He watches it bounce one, two, three times before it sinks. "Great way to start the weekend, isn't it?"

"But you never said…"

He smiles sadly. "I didn't want to talk about it as it was – never mind talk about the talking about it. I'm just saying. If *you* wanted to…"

I can't answer. Not quite. Not without sounding like a hamster on speed. So I do the only thing I can, and I rest my head against his shoulder. He tips his head sideways so it rests against mine and we stare out at the water.

"Do you have to go, Steff?"

"Yeah. I have to go."

"I don't want you to."

"Course you don't. Who the hell's going to teach you to drive?"

"Oh, I don't know. Someone who can *actually* drive, maybe?"


"Aren't you scared?"

We're sitting back at the side of the cliff. The tide has come in further, and because *someone* made us move, we no longer have to worry about getting cut off. The sun is starting to dip towards the water, but there's still time before it sets. We've been here all afternoon, but somehow it feels like it's only been an hour.

Steffan considers my question. He's peeling the label off his beer bottle; slowly shredding it and scattering the pieces onto the sand. "What's the point?" he says after a while. "It's like Mum said – the only things worth being scared of are the things you can do something about. Then there's a point to it – you can be frightened of doing the wrong thing, you can be frightened of making the wrong choice – but when you don't have a choice, why waste your energy on worrying about what you can't control?"

It sounds like the kind of thing his mum used to say. She was always so calm – even when she was dying.

Especially when she was dying.

And look what she's left him – look at her legacy. Words

he can live by, words he *believes* in. Something that keeps him looking ahead and stops him from getting lost. Even now, she's his lighthouse, his beacon.

I envy that, I think. Alone in the dark.

I know he wants to help – is trying to, because that's who he is – but I think he only has enough light for one, and I won't be the one to take it. Like I said, I want to find the way myself – not just try to retrace his steps.

Jared is leaning back on his elbows, his legs stretched out on the sand in front of him. "You know what scares me?"

"Earwigs." Steffan and I say it together. Jared pulls a face.

"Other than earwigs." He takes a swig of his beer – the only one he's had – and narrows his eyes. "That deep down, I'm just like him."

There can only be one "him". Jared's dad. It's in the tone of his voice – even in the way his lip curls when he says the word. Everything you need to know about the way Jared feels about his father you can read right there on his face.

I don't think it was always that way – I mean, I know enough to know that Jared's love of cars comes from his dad, so there must have been *something* between them. Not that you'd know it now.

He leans across to Steffan and hands him what's left of his beer. There's at least two thirds of the bottle left, and I can see Steffan's torn between taking it and not. He's had a few of his own already – which is why Jared's not even finished his first. Someone's got to drive the car, haven't they?

"Sloppy seconds?" Steffan shakes his head. Jared shrugs and, with a flick of his wrist, he upends the bottle. Beer pours out onto the sand and drains away.

It feels like they're waiting for something. It hangs in the air. They're waiting...for me. It's part of the game, isn't it? Where they go, I follow. What are we afraid of? Steffan answers the question by avoiding it. Jared gives you a piece of a puzzle you didn't even know needed solving. And I...

Well, I'm the talker, aren't I? But this, even I can't say – not out loud. This is one of those things you keep to yourself and you turn over in the quiet, dark hours and you bite your lip and wish it would go away.

What am I afraid of? Anyone could tell you that; the list goes on and on. Spiders, snakes. Flying. Being hit by a falling satellite. Car crashes. Exams (specifically *failing* them). Being late. Being forgotten. Being lost. Cannibals. Serial killers. Axe murderers. (Although those last three quite often overlap, from what I can gather, so if we count those as one thing the list looks a little more respectable...)

But what scares me – what really scares me – is the thing I can't get out of my head. It's the one single thing that bothers me more than anything else – more than

186

anything else ever has – and of course it's to do with my mother.

My greatest fear, my one *real* fear, is that she was awake. I am so afraid that she was awake as she died; that she knew what was happening to her. That she was afraid, and horrified, and helpless.

Steffan's mother may have been able to separate fear and death. She had time. She had months of staring them both in the face – what else could she do? She found strength in meeting them head-on and if she was afraid she hid it from her son, because that's what a mother does.

At least, that's what a mother does if she knows what's coming.

Did *mine* know what was coming? I wonder. In the end, did she? I hope, with every piece of me that she didn't. I hope that there wasn't time for her to know. I hope that it was over before she could even know it had begun.

I hope.

# eighteen

Steffan has hit the dozy phase. It's one of his most annoying habits. A couple of beers and he turns into a cat. Not literally, obviously. That would be weird. But he starts yawning and getting bleary-eyed and looking for a quiet spot to settle down and...yeah. It's annoying.

It's especially annoying when you're in a small metal shoebox of a car and he's trying to rest his head on your shoulder and use you as a pillow. As he is right now. Why he climbed into the back seat with me, I'll never know. The other half of the seat's covered with all his junk, but it doesn't seem to bother him; he just sat himself down on top of it all, and now he's doing his best to fall asleep.

"Jared?"

"Mmm?"

"Stop the car, will you?"

Jared pulls over as far as he can on what's essentially a

single-track lane – he's almost in the hedge. It's the only road in or out of the Havens and if anyone else comes along we're screwed. I could have stayed there until it got dark, but we can't exactly sleep on the beach, can we? Besides, there wasn't any more food, so.

Jared turns round in the driver's seat to look at me. "You alright?"

"Do I look alright?" I point at Steffan. He's snoring. That took about a minute and a half. He's moments away from starting to dribble on my shoulder.

"Mmm." He waits while I slide out from beneath Steffan's head (why's it so heavy, anyway? It's not like he's got a brain in there) and clamber forward into the passenger seat.

I can open the window here. You have no idea how exciting this is. I wind it all the way down, then halfway back up again. And then all the way back down.

Jared stares at me with barely disguised amusement.

"Window," I say as nonchalantly as I can. "It goes up and down."

"You done?"

"I'm done."

We both glance into the back, where Steffan has arranged himself in the corner, draped over a sleeping bag, mumbling slightly.

"Shall we leave him behind?" Jared asks, not entirely joking.

"Tempting," I say, watching him snuggle more closely into the crumpled sleeping bag. "Could just take a photo of him and put it on Facebook…"

"He'll love that…"

"Serve him right, won't it?"

"You're still pissed he dropped you in the sea."

"Yes, I am." I hold up my phone, framing him in the camera screen and pressing the button. There's a fake shutter noise and a tiny version of Steffan shrinks until he's smaller than my fingernail, then spins off down to the left-hand corner of the screen. Steffan, frozen in time. Asleep, just as he is now. That version of him will remain, always. No matter what happens to him or to me or to Jared. No one can take that away. (Well, obviously they can take my phone or something, I suppose. I mean more that the moment's there. If you catch my drift.)

I am settling into my seat – front seat, no less – when there's an ominous "clonk" from somewhere in the car. Jared's eyebrow shoots up. He looks at me. I look at him. The snoring in the back continues.

Clonk.

"Was that the engine?" I ask.

"I'm…not sure." But he turns the ignition off anyway, killing the engine. We sit quietly, listening. Waiting.

I can hear Jared breathing; the steady, slow rise and fall of his breath. I can see his chest moving up and down, in and out. If I put my hand flat against his skin, just there, I would be able to feel his heart beating under my palm. Would it be slow and rhythmic like his breathing? Or would it race and skip like mine has taken to doing every time I look at him? Would his heart speed up beneath my touch, or would he step back, step away and give me that shuttered-eye look that I've seen him give so many other people? Would Jared let me in? I wonder. Is that what I want, or am I just flailing around in the dark, reaching for the first thing I can hold on to?

Jared is, after all, Jared.

There's a loud snort from the back seat, making us both jump...and immediately afterwards, there's another clonk.

"Is it him?" I whisper, pointing back towards Steffan. Jared frowns; shakes his head. He points up. He's pointing to the car roof.

I left something off my list of stuff that I'm scared of. Along with the serial killers / cannibals / mad axemen, there's Men With Hooks From Urban Legends. You know the ones. In particular, the Maniac With A Hook Who Bangs On The Top Of The Car And Then There's A Head There And Oh My God We're All Going To Die Screaming. That one.

Clonk.

I look up at the roof. "Do not like."

"You realize that if it was a psycho with a hook, he'd

have hauled you out through your window already, right?" Jared laughs, pointing to the open window.

Please, oh please, just let it be that he knows me well enough to know I'm thinking about Hook Man, and not that I'm actually saying everything that crosses my mind out loud. Because with the heartbeats and the breathing and the...oh god, that would be embarrassing. I'm embarrassed just contemplating the possibility.

I wind the window up.

Clonk.

Jared is out of his door before I can blink. He moves around the front of the car, and I can see the grin spreading across his face. He bangs on the bonnet and mouths something about getting out of the car. He's pointing at the roof.

So, no Hook Man then?

Clonk.

This one's loud enough to startle Steffan awake, and through the windscreen I can see Jared starting to laugh. He's waving for me to come and look.

"What the hell was that noise?" Steffan's gone from snoring to wide awake and stroppy in about three seconds, and is trying to haul himself into the front between the seats. That can't end well.

I get out of the car, clambering across the driver's seat to the door. There's no way I'll get mine open.

I stand in front of the car and look at the roof.

"You have got to be kidding me."

An elephant this morning…and now this?

Two large round eyes blink back at me. There's also a beak, and a very long neck which is attached to a body on the other side of the hedge.

It's an ostrich.

Steffan follows me out of the car, takes one look at me and then at the enormous bird peering over the hedge at us and says (with characteristic charm), "Holy shit."

The ostrich responds by pecking the roof of the car again.

Clonk.

"Oi!" Steffan's voice goes up an octave.

Clonk.

"Stop hitting my car, would you?"

Clonk.

I can't hold it back any longer. I am utterly, hopelessly, helpless with laughter. There is an ostrich peering over the hedge at us on a tiny little road just up from the beach and it is pecking Steffan's car and he's getting angry with it. He's shouting at an ostrich.

Another head pops up just along the hedge.

"Umm, Steff…?" Jared's pointing at it.

And then there's another one. And another. They're all blinking at us – except the one pecking the roof of the car, which seems to have entered into some kind of furious stare-down with Steffan.

"Where are we?" I ask, looking from ostrich to ostrich. It feels like a perfectly sensible question.

"Look." Jared has spotted the sign, hanging there casually above the fence just up the road. "Seaview Ostrich Farm," he reads.

An ostrich farm. Seriously?

Then it clicks. "Loads of the hotels round here have ostrich meat on the menu in their restaurants, don't they?" I ask. Jared shrugs. Steffan's still busy glaring down a really big bird. "There was a thing in the paper about it. This is where it comes from!"

"Ostrich farm? Are you messing with me?" Steffan doesn't even blink. His opponent, however, appears to be backing down. The head disappears back behind the hedge. The other ostrich heads follow it.

The hedge isn't especially tall, but it's growing on a steep verge. Which means the top of it's well above our heads – but the idea of there being an entire field of ostriches on the other side of it is, frankly, too wacky to pass up. I smack Steffan on the arm.

"Give me a boost, would you?"

"Not bloody likely, Lim."

"Well, I can either sit on your shoulders or I can climb on your car. Which would you rather? Either way, I'm looking over that hedge."

He takes a moment to weigh up his options.

Two minutes later, I'm balanced precariously on his shoulders, wobbling towards the hedge.

"Uh...wow."

On the other side of the hedge is – as the sign suggested – an ostrich farm. The field, which is mostly rough, tussocky grass, stretches away and down towards the sea; from here, it almost looks as though it drops straight into the water. There is nothing but the sparkling blue, catching the early evening sun, and the dusty heat-yellowed green of the grass. And there are the ostriches. Obviously.

I can see maybe a dozen of them, wandering around aimlessly. They look odd, all legs and neck; so out of place here. Somehow, they belong and yet they don't, and I can't quite put my finger on the how or the why of it.

"What's it like?" Steffan slaps my knee with the back of his hand. He's obviously bored of not dropping me.

"Oh, you know. Ostrich-y."

"Ostrich-y."

"It's a word."

"Sure. So, can I put you down now – because you're—"

"Don't even think about saying it." I nudge the side of his ribs with my foot. "You may put me down, good sir. Gently."

"Thank Christ for that." He drops into an awkward crouch, and my feet touch the surface of the road.

"Ostrich-y," I say again with a shrug, straightening

myself out. My clothes still feel slightly damp in places and they cling to me. The heat of the day has turned sticky, almost as though there's a storm on the way – but the sky is clear, even out over the sea. If there's a storm coming, it's hiding itself well.

"Where's he gone now?" Steffan is looking around. Jared has vanished.

"Eaten by ostriches, mate," says a voice from the hedge, and Jared's head pops out of the middle of it. "There's a hole in the hedge."

"We're not going in there. No way," I say, hoping I sound firm and authoritative and, well, sensible.

"Why not?" asks the hedge.

"Because it's…a farm. And there's a hedge and a sign and basically it's trespassing."

"So?"

"Also, ostriches. Can't they break your arm or something?" I sound less firm now. More desperate.

"Only if you give them a reason to. I just want a look that doesn't involve having to sit on his shoulders. Besides, it's not like we're going to try and ride them or anything, is it?"

Steffan, hearing this, suddenly looks thoughtful.

"No," I say.

He looks wounded. "Thought never even crossed my mind," he says.

Like I believe that.

We both peer through the gap in the hedge. Jared is through, standing in the field. His back is to us, and he's silhouetted against the sparkling sea; his hands at his sides. Several of the ostriches are walking towards him, obviously expecting him to feed them. Either that or they're getting ready to eat him. I won't lie: it's a bit creepy. One comes close enough for him to touch – and slowly, slowly, he raises his hand, gently setting it on the bird's back. It turns to look at him and blinks. He takes his hand away again.

I can feel my heart pounding in my throat. What if it had decided to attack him? What if it hadn't been tame (well, tame-ish)? What if, instead of seeing his touch as friendly, as curious, as harmless, it had decided to rip his hand off? How did he know that it wouldn't – and why would he be nuts enough to risk it?

And then it occurs to me that he's risking getting his hand torn off because he wants to. Because he thinks the risk is worth the reward.

"You done being the Ostrich Whisperer?" Steffan calls. He's not impressed; standing there with his arms crossed, he's obviously not forgiven any of them for pecking his car roof. Not that one more dent would make a difference to the Rust Bucket, but I know better than to point this out. Has anyone ever had a blood feud with a bird? Because this looks like it could be the first.

"Yeah, yeah," says Jared, turning around to face us.

He's smiling. Not grinning; it goes deeper than that. He looks *happy*. Like whatever he was thinking has washed everything else away, wiped his mind clean. He looks different, somehow. And when his eyes meet mine, they hold my gaze and without knowing when it happened, or how, or why, I'm smiling too.

# nineteen

"Wait. An actual bed?" I can't quite believe what I'm hearing. That whole "on the road, staying in tents" thing lasted about as long as a packet of crisps near Jared. Not exactly surprising, knowing Steffan (whatever he says). I'm relieved. Granted, it's only been one night since I slept in a bed – my bed – but somehow, the idea of Not Having To Sleep In A Tent Tonight is already exotic. Maybe because time has twisted and stretched since I walked out of my front door. Maybe because I have. Although perhaps I'm not so much twisting as bouncing back. Rewinding and replaying. Rebounding. Becoming what I was before, but more.

For better or for worse; the same but different.

The hostel was Steffan's idea. I *knew* he'd crack; him with his "Yeah, sure, we're camping." He might have been a Scout, but that was a long time ago – and when he saw the hostel, right down by the beach in the next village along the coast, he made such a big fuss from the passenger seat (yes, I've been relegated to the back again – what can you do?) that Jared didn't really have any choice other than to pull over. I wonder whether the hostel being slap bang next to one of the best pubs round this way – and one which happens to be a bit flimsy on the ID policy in the summer – has anything to do with it. Not that I'm a cynic or anything, you understand...

This is the surfing sweet-spot of the coast – hence the hostel, and the astonishing predictability of a whole row of old VW camper vans parked up along the road with boards leaning against them – not to mention the townies sitting on the benches outside the pub, wetsuits rolled down to their waists, dripping gently onto the pavement. I swear I just saw one of them shake a head full of (bleached) hair back, braying something about "the lifestyle, man". Yeah, right.

Alright for some, isn't it? The ones who can just load themselves into a van and drive off into the sunset when the mood takes them. The ones who can come and go as they please – who can get out if they want to. But then, looking at them and listening to them, I guess the trade-off for having that particular "lifestyle" is to be an insufferable wanker, so it's all a question of balance.

While Steffan and Jared attempt to deploy their considerable charm at the hostel to get us beds for the night (and when I say "charm", I mean it in the loosest possible sense; ditto "considerable") I cross the road and sit on the wall above the beach, dangling my feet over. There's a big drop here; the slipway's further along, and beneath me is the part of the beach where all the dinghies are tied up, far above the reach of the high waterline. They're used for sailing lessons, mostly by kids, and usually they're busy all summer long – but looking down at them now, I don't think some have been in the water for a long time. They're high and dry and safe on the shore – but that's not what boats are built for, is it? For waiting, for staying safe. They're meant for sailing; meant to be out on the waves.

Amy has sent me a text message. It's brief and to the point, and tells me nothing more and nothing less than I was expecting.

*Dad in2 treatment 2morrow. 6 weeks residential. Will take him. U want to stay with me? Let me know when ur coming back. xx A*

That word again. Treatment. Weirdly, the first thing I think about is his office. I wonder if everyone he works with knows. I wonder if they already did. Would hearing this be a relief to them? Some of the people from his work came to the funeral and they were almost as careful not to get too close to him as they were to be polite to me.

But...*treatment.*

Maybe it isn't too late for him. Maybe I should take that as a sign – as some kind of encouragement. Maybe.

The sun is finally on its way down into the water. It looks like it's hovering right above the surface, just hanging there – and the evening has brought a calm that's still enough for the sea to reflect it perfectly. In the bay ahead of me there are two suns: one sinking into the waves as its twin rises to meet it...and then they're both gone.

I half-wonder whether Jared wants company on his Great American Journey; whether Steffan can smuggle us both out in his suitcase when he leaves. Everything here feels such a mess. Can you blame me for wanting to run?

There's laughter behind me, and footsteps, and then someone shoves a ratty piece of laminated paper in front of me.

"Dinner, isn't it?" says Steffan, dropping into a slouch beside me and swinging his leg over the sea wall. Jared follows a moment later – but oddly, he doesn't sit on the other side of Steffan. He sits, much to my surprise, on the other side of *me*. This is...unusual. It makes me momentarily forget what I'm meant to be doing. I look blankly at the paper Steff just handed me, then at Steff. He looks blankly back at me.

"What?" he says.

"What?" I say.

"Food?" He taps the front of the sheet, and I finally get

202

myself together enough to actually look at it. The word MENU is printed in wonky capital letters across the top.

Dinner. Right. Yes. So, not expecting me to eat the paper, then. Good.

"Let me guess. Pie?" I hand the sheet back to him. They both make appreciative noises. After all, it can only be a matter of half an hour since they scoffed that pack of chicken wings that had somehow got left in the car. (Meat sitting in a hot car all afternoon? I passed, thanks.)

"Not having the ostrich steak?" It's still funny. It is.

"I'm not sure Jared should – you know, not now he's bonded with them and everything. It'd be like eating one of his own." The slight wobble in Steffan's voice gives away just how hard he's trying to keep a straight face. Jared nods calmly, chucking a pebble down onto the beach. He manages to hit one of the dinghies. There's a fibreglassy clonk.

"Whoops." Jared glances around to see whether anyone heard.

Only me.

Even Steffan's too busy pawing at the menu. You'd think he was a starving man, looking at him: he's reading every single thing on there – even though he knows as well as I do that he'll order a pie, because given the choice between pie and anything else in this world (untold riches! Wisdom beyond the reach of men!) he will *always* choose pie. The pie always wins.

It feels fake somehow, this. Like we're playing at being grown-ups. Frauds. And maybe we are: just playing. But I don't feel like *I'm* a fake. Yet here we are, sitting on a wall and ordering dinner from a pub like civilized people.

Mind you, the second I think this, Steff lets out an almighty great belch and sniffs loudly. "Beer," he says, and rubs his hands together.

"You're disgusting."

"Better out than in." He looks revoltingly pleased with himself. Almost as revolting is the faint waft of cigar smoke that's still lingering around him like a cloud of cartoon flies. I flap my hand dramatically and he rolls his eyes.

"Such a grouch," he says.

"Steff?" I say sweetly, leaning back to look at him as he stands up, menu in hand. He raises an eyebrow at me. "Scampi?" I bat my eyelashes in what I hope is an adorable, irresistible manner.

"You want to get that looked at," he says, tapping the edge of the menu against the flat of his palm. "Might have conjunctivitis."

"Funny."

"I know." He grins and ducks over the road and into the pub.

Behind us, one of the bar staff is bringing out lanterns to set on the tables clustered around the front of the pub.

She's got an armful of them, and we half-turn to watch her weaving between the surfers and the locals and a group who look like they're pretty much exactly the same as us, and are probably staying in the hostel too. There's a clatter as she drops one – and before I can even blink, Jared's off the wall and across the road and is helping her pick it up; taking the others off her and setting them on the end of the nearest table for her to light. The bleach-blond-wetsuit-surfer-boys were right next to her and not a single one of them moved.

And what's that sudden sour spike I can feel, somewhere inside my chest? It feels a lot like jealousy, but it can't be that. Not when Jared is simply being Jared. But he smiles at her and says something that's too quiet for me to hear, and she laughs and hands him a lantern, and suddenly there's fingernails raking down the inside of my ribs.

I think it's fair to say that this is an overreaction. Just a teeny one.

The real shock, though, is that I feel anything at all. Because this is Jared, and...

And this is Jared.

And.

And.

"You alright?" Jared asks, sitting back down on the wall. He sets the lantern down between us and the little flame inside it flickers, then straightens and steadies.

"Me? Oh, sure." I slide my hands underneath my knees so he can't see them shaking.

Because this is Jared, and suddenly I understand.

"How's the hand?"

There's still no sign of Steffan. He's got talking to someone, that's my guess. Steffan attracts conversation; he just has one of those faces, one of those demeanours. The kind of general Steffan-ness which suggests to people that yes, he'd love to stop for a chat. The thing is, he usually would. It's fine. I'm used to it.

"The hand?" Jared's question takes me by surprise. I actually hold both hands up and look at them as though, up till that point, I'd forgotten what "a hand" is. I realize how stupid this looks and put my hands back down again.

"Is it sore?" Jared nods towards my right hand.

Ah. He means after I walloped Becca.

Was that only yesterday? It feels like weeks ago. Months. And if that was yesterday, the funeral was only the day before. How does that work? Already it feels like it was so long ago that it may as well have been another lifetime. Like it happened to someone else.

I wonder if it did.

I'm different, I think. I didn't feel it happen, didn't see it – but something in me has changed. Amy's text about my father might have broken the me of two days ago: the Funeral Limpet, who was pretending so hard to be something she was not. She was the thin ice over the winter river; the single glass sheet that covers the deepest well. I am…something else. Someone else.

There are no ghosts. Nothing looming over me; not now. And somewhere in the distance, far ahead of me in the dark, I can see a light.

A single lantern, with a little flame that flickers and then steadies.

Cracked and crazed I may still be, but maybe – just maybe – the cracks are showing signs of growing smaller. Not by much, not yet, but give them time.

Perhaps I'm not made of glass after all. Perhaps I'm made of something stronger.

I know. I'm as shocked by that thought as you are.

"My hand? Oh, yeah, it's fine," I mumble, rubbing at my knuckles. And it is, which presumably proves that I hit like a girl. What were you expecting?

"You could've broken something."

"Yeah, Becca's face. What a loss *that* would've been."

He doesn't answer, but when I look round, he's watching me. His eyes are searching my face; taking in every part of it. Drinking me in. He's still sitting there, silent, watching me, when Steffan reappears.

"How the hell can you see anything?" he says, setting

down a small round metal tray with glasses on it. "Twinkly bloody lanterns, my arse. It's too dark."

"It's called night, Steff. You see, when the sun goes to bed…"

"Alright, Limpet. Don't get smart or I won't tell you what just happened."

"You went in to order food and got lost? You had to go and hunt down the cow for your pie all by yourself?"

Jared joins in. "Cow? Don't know why you bothered – there's a whole load of ostriches up on the hill…"

We dissolve into giggles. Steffan tries to scowl – but his frown breaks and he starts shaking his head and laughing. "And I suppose we'll be using you as bait, will we?"

"At least they like *me*," Jared laughs.

"Let's see you being smug about it when they're eating you, right?"

"Are you planning on throwing me to them whole, or just feeding them my dismembered limbs?"

"Not sure yet." Steffan takes a swig of his drink and wags a finger across me at Jared. "Sleep with one eye open, boyo."

"Enough!" I hold up my hands in surrender. "What's this amazing thing that you were threatening to not tell us?" I nudge Steffan, who lurches sideways in an attempt not to spill his drink. Jared – automatically forgiven, as always – reaches across me and clicks his fingers impatiently until Steff passes him a glass.

"So you know how Gethin has a band?"

"How could we forget?" I finally get my drink.

The saga of Gethin's Band is an epic, sprawling tale of love, betrayal and a crashing inability to find a drummer who can keep time...reaching as far back as the days when Steffan and Jared were in football club with him. Since then, Gethin's band has been through good times (their demo getting played by one of the new music DJs in Cardiff) and bad (pretty much all the rest of it). Lately, though, they appear to have got themselves together and have even been playing *in public*. Once or twice, members of said public have even *paid for the privilege of hearing them* – which I'm sure is as much of a shock to Gethin and company as it is to the rest of us.

The long and the short of Steff's news is that somehow (I suspect massive bribery on the part of Gethin's father), the band have found themselves on the bill of a not-insignificant local music festival, tomorrow night... The catch being that, technically, said festival is supposed to be vaguely folk-flavoured. Gethin, in his wisdom, has decided that the way around this is to have someone play the violin onstage with them.

Guess who he's asked?

# twenty

Even after a heavy dose of pub pie and beer, Steffan's still feeling far too hyped up and sociable to even think about sleeping. So while I would happily have voted for bed (a bed! Even a crappy hostel bed!) instead, we're watching the surfers build a beach bonfire. Well, I tell a lie. Jared and I are watching them, sitting in an old fibreglass dinghy a little way along the beach, while Steffan buzzes about being the life and soul of the party. Maybe he just doesn't want to go to bed, because if he goes to bed and closes his eyes, when he opens them it'll be tomorrow, and however exciting this festival thing might be, however hard he's trying not to think about it, there's the minor matter of his mother's grave to think about first – not a million miles along the road from here.

The surfers are – as you'd expect from a bunch of show-off lifestylers, as opposed to proper surfers (I'll stop now, honest) – pretty bloody useless, and burning logs keep falling off the top of the pile they've built, only to be kicked back in by whoever happens to be closest to them. Predictably, they're all wearing sandals, so I'm figuring there's a lot of burned toes happening. Jared snorts with amusement every now and again – I think he's hoping one of them falls in.

Occasionally, I catch a glimpse of Steffan, beer in hand, the firelight flickering across his face. He looks happy enough for now, and I'm glad.

Jared's sitting at the other end of the dinghy, with the glow of the fire catching the curve of his brow, his nose, his cheekbones. His legs are stretched out along the inside of the boat, his feet almost touching mine. Whoever the dinghy belongs to, they're lucky it hasn't rained in a while: most summers, a boat left the right way up on the beach would be full of water in a couple of days. It would sit there, going gently green inside. As it is, it's full of sand and shells; someone's even tried to build a tiny sandcastle between the narrow plastic planks that serve as seats. One tower remains, slumped sideways across itself. A tiny paper flag is still sticking out of the ramparts at a wacky angle. Go home, castle, you're drunk.

There's a shuffling sound in the sand nearby and we both look over – just in time to see Surfer Dude Number Four throwing up emphatically behind an abandoned windbreak. At least, I really hope it's abandoned – or there's a family in for a nasty surprise when they toddle on down to the beach tomorrow. Surfer Dude surveys his handiwork, wipes his mouth with the back of his hand and sets off back towards the bonfire. It's a circuitous route, given he can't even walk in a straight line, and he stops every few steps to take a swig from the bottle he's still holding.

Closer to the fire, there are raised voices. A scuffle. Sound and fury; fists. Always the same. Bruises and regret.

The sound of breaking glass somewhere close by makes me jump – and suddenly Jared's hand is on my shoulder.

"Hey…" It's all he says.

The bottle of beer I was holding lies smashed at my feet; the remains of my drink bubble away into the base of the boat and around the sad little sandcastle, forming a frothing white moat.

"Why do they do it?" I ask. "What's it for? Like that guy…" I wave in the direction of Surfer Dude – who, after an epic journey, has almost made it back to the safety of the firelight. As we watch, he slumps onto the sand, still waving his bottle.

"Because." The boat creaks as Jared shifts his weight. "They do it because."

"Because? That's it?"

"I'm not the one to ask, am I? And besides, you're not really asking why *they* drink, are you?"

212

"I guess not."

I picture Becca, sneering at me. I picture us, the three of us, sitting up on the hill by the pillbox. I picture Jared, carrying a lantern and setting it down between us and I figure it's okay.

"You know about my mother, right?"

And I tell him. I tell him about the drink. I tell him about the slurring and the forgetting and the falling down stairs. I tell him about the nights I had to put her to bed because she couldn't do it herself. I tell him about all the times I was the parent and she was the child. I tell him about the bottles hidden around the house: in wardrobes and cupboards and tucked into corners. I tell him the truth of it – because what's the point in pretending? I tell him all the things I've carried with me, quiet and close, the things I couldn't bear to think about, let alone say out loud; the things I didn't even realize I had words for – and I know I can, because of the pillbox and the shower block and Barley Vale; because of the lantern; because of the bonfire and the night and the sound of the waves on the beach. The fire burns it and the darkness smothers it and the waves wash it all away.

He sits and listens and I talk and I talk and I talk and it's all pouring out of me suddenly. Things I've never told anyone; not Amy, not Steff. No one. And now I'm telling Jared and I can't stop. Might as well try to stop the tide going out. Might as well try and hold the whole beach in my hands.

I tell him about the fights. About the time I came home and found both my parents drunk and bruised and my father telling me to pick a side. I tell him how my dad locked all the doors and sat down at the table; how he hid my phone and pulled the landline out of the wall and how my mother just sat on the floor and stared into space. How I climbed out of the window and ran to our neighbours, and how he's never forgiven me yet. Did I pick the right side? I wonder. Was there ever going to be one? I couldn't say, because *this* doesn't feel like winning.

I tell him how I know everyone in town knows about the drinking. How they probably knew long before me. How it's unfair that a town which thinks it's fun to go out on a Friday night and get collectively hammered can stand and point fingers on a Monday morning. The sheer injustice of the comments behind my back. The whispers I didn't pick up on until it was too late, and I can't decide if I wish I had noticed them sooner. Because you shouldn't wish for things you wouldn't like. But what would I rather: that people in our stupid little town, where everyone knows everybody else's business before they know it themselves, were laughing at my mother, or at me? Which is worse? To be the one at fault or the one tainted by someone else's mistakes?

And when the flood subsides and I don't have the words any more, I stop. I have to. The light from the bonfire casts long, distorted shadows and if I squint I can just about make out Steffan with his arm slung around the shoulder of one of the surfer dudes. He's still laughing, and I'm sure I can smell cigars. He's obviously been making friends and handing out the rest of the box. Good riddance, I say. They're vile things, and not nearly as cool as he thinks they are (although naturally the surfers think they're The Best Thing Ever). Every now and again, the fire flares blue and green, shooting up sparks from the salt in the burning driftwood.

Jared waits the longest time, and then I hear him sigh. He rolls his empty bottle between the palms of his hands. The glass catches the light from the bonfire and glitters between his fingers. Grains of sand fall to the floor of the boat like stardust. "Can I tell you something?" he says, and it's not really a question. It's a plea; a prayer for absolution. Jared's opening the shutters, unlocking the doors. Letting the mask drop – even if it's only by a fraction.

"Sure."

"You won't like it."

"Oh."

What's he going to tell me? He's already with someone. He's with Becca. Ha! No. Not that. But what if…what if he tells me that he's had enough and he's leaving too? That

Steffan leaving, that his mother and her newly-planned life without him, they're all it takes for him to shrug and pack his bags and disappear. What if he's leaving too? What if, what if – what if I lose them both?

He's watching me. Waiting for me to put my listening face on. I'm sure I have one; I've always used it in chemistry, even when I haven't got a clue what the hell is going on around me. Maybe it's not my Listening Face so much as my...*actual* face. Just my face. Still. It'll have to do. I arrange my face into what I hope looks like the kind of face someone who's listening would wear, and I listen. After all, he's listened to me, hasn't he?

"It was at the funeral. Your mum's," he adds – just in case I don't know which one he means. "At the funeral, in the church. I was thinking about you..."

(Oh really? No. Stop it. *Listening Face*.)

"...and I was thinking about Steff..."

(Ah. Bugger. Stand down, soldier.)

"...and about his mum's funeral..."

(Well. That escalated quickly...)

"...and about how life would go if mine wasn't here any more either."

(Don't wish for things you wouldn't like, Jared. Sound advice there. I even gave it to myself about three minutes ago.)

"I know it sounds bad. It's just...I don't know."

"'Bad' is one way of putting it, yes."

"Forget it. Forget I said anything, alright?" He's still rolling the bottle between his hands – faster now, back and forth, back and forth. Listening Face didn't do the trick, obviously. My hands have gone cold and hot at the same time, and there's a lump in my throat. I swallow it back down and I curl my fingers into fists because *look at him*. Rolling the bottle between his hands, his head down and looking like he's all alone in the world. There's a reason he's telling me this and not Steffan – and much as I'd love to think it's because he felt the same thing I did earlier on the wall, I know he's telling me because he doesn't think he can tell Steffan.

Why doesn't he think he can tell Steffan?

He feels like he's all alone, and he needs someone to show him that's not true.

"It's not just my mum," he says, and thank god the Listening Face seems to be holding up. "It's my dad too. If they were gone – just gone – then there wouldn't be all this. I'd be free, wouldn't I? I wouldn't be their kid. I'd just be me. Whoever that's supposed to be." He says the last part with a laugh; tries to hide it behind his hand as he rubs his jaw.

Who are any of us supposed to be? That's the big question, isn't it?

"It's like you said – everybody talking about you and

217

your family, everyone whispering behind your back. I know that. I know how it feels. Every single day – only it's not just Becca bloody Roberts, is it? It's the local paper. It's the news. It's Dad being hauled out of the house by the police *again*, and this time he's stolen from everyone you know. From your friends. And you have to walk past them every day. You've got classes with them the day after he's sentenced."

"He's coming back, though. Maybe you should try and patch it up."

"I don't want to patch it up."

"He's your dad…"

"He's a liar and a thief and an all-round shit, Lim." He lowers his eyes, drops his voice until I can barely hear it over the sound of the waves on the beach. "Besides, I'm not you."

"What's that supposed to mean?"

"It means that you're the one who would be able to do that. You're better than this. Better than me."

"Am I interrupting?" Steffan's timing remains *impeccable*. He swings himself into the beached boat with a grin, his voice a little too loud.

"Bit late to ask now, isn't it?" Jared mumbles, turning his face away.

Steffan's eyebrow shoots up. "Oh, is it?" He makes a clicking sound out of the corner of his mouth. I wish I didn't know what that meant, but I do. Bloody Steffan.

"Shut up, Steff." Everything feels taut; strained somehow. Stretched. Like we're all holding back, pulling our punches. There's something in here with us. Something else. Not one of our attendant ghosts; it has too much weight, too much bulk for that. Something that can do more damage than a ghost. A secret.

"So, what are we talking about?" He leans back slightly and tries to put his feet up on the side of the boat. He misses and his legs drop down with a thump, knocking the remains of the sandcastle over. RIP castle. We barely knew you. Steffan's trying to figure out what to do with his feet now he can't put them up, and Jared's mood is sinking fast again. I can feel it pulling us all down with it, just like in Barley Vale.

Barley Vale, where Jared said he wanted to see what his father had done; where he realized that it was all still *there*. To see that the rust might be setting in, but the foundations were still strong: chipped and damaged but still standing.

Barley Vale, where Steffan pulled away and gave him that look that was so unlike him. So unlike *them*.

Something I've not seen. Something I've been missing.

Steffan, so reluctant to tell us he's leaving. Steffan, who's been my best friend for years. Steffan, who's known Jared for ever.

Jared, who is so angry with his father. Jared, on edge and so guilty and always standing back watching and listening and...

Something I've missed because I've been caught up in my own head. In my grief. Tangled in this strange dark thing with teeth and claws and a thousand thousand blinding-black scales.

"Steffan," I say, and my voice is small. "Why are you leaving really?"

# twenty-one

There's a silence in our little boat. It's thick and it's heavy and it comes between us like a curtain. We are three people all adrift, lost at sea – even on the sand. We are alone, however together we might seem.

Steffan shifts on his narrow seat. "Why am I going?"

"Why are you going?"

"Told you. Dad. Headhunted. All that." He waves an arm at the night.

"Bollocks." Why couldn't I see it before? Lying, lying, lying. He might be telling the truth about the job, the headhunting – but that's not all of it. That's why I couldn't see it: a partial truth is so much easier to pass than a whole lie.

"You want to know?"

"No. I'm asking for fun. Of course I want to know!"

"Ask him." He jerks his thumb towards Jared, who

crumples inside. I see it happen. It's not the look on his face, which stays just the same. It's the way he holds his shoulders, the way he carries himself.

"Don't," he says quietly.

Steffan scowls. "She asked."

I'm on the verge of telling them both to grow up – mostly because they're *both* scaring me now – when Jared cracks.

"They're broke," he says quietly. There is nothing beyond the boat but the sand and the stars and the faltering light from the bonfire. "They're broke because he took it all."

I don't need to ask who he means.

It explains a lot: the odd looks between them, the half-sentences. Why Steffan's left it until he's as good as gone before he tells us he's leaving. Why Barley Vale meant so much to Jared, and why Steffan was so unlike himself. It might have made Jared feel better, but how did it help Steff?

"You're broke?" I turn towards him.

He throws his arms wide and flops backwards, banging his head on the side of the boat. "Broke as a very, very broke thing."

"But…the house…"

"Not ours any more."

"Your dad's car?"

"Nope."

(I decide not to remind either of them that the last time anyone saw the keys for that, Jared was lobbing them into the pond.)

"Your car?"

"Christ, you don't think anyone'd actually want that thing, do you?" He's right about that: even I wouldn't want the Rust Bucket – not unless you disinfected every centimetre of it, and then nuked it just to be sure. Some of the crap he keeps in there is...well, it's unsanitary.

"You're not going to lose your violin, are you?"

"No." He sounds pretty sure. "That's mine. All part of my inheritance, remember? Anyway, who's going to be brave enough to try and take that away? Doesn't scan well, does it: bailiffs take away son's treasured violin, bought with his dead mother's legacy..." He presses a hand to his forehead.

"Would you just stop?" Jared snaps. "Stop."

"What's your problem?" Steff asks, sitting up again. "It's not like you're having to leave, is it? It's not like your friend's dad came along and took *your* dad for everything he had – and then some; it's not like you went into your mate's house and looked around and wondered exactly what had been bought with your mum's life insurance, is it? It's not like it happened to you, so what's your problem?"

"Steff!" I'm appalled at how casually cruel he's being. It's more than the words, it's the sound of them. The feel

223

of them. The feeling *behind* them. No wonder Jared couldn't talk to him about his dad.

Why didn't I know this? Why didn't Steffan tell me? Why've I been so thick that I couldn't see it before now?

Steffan catches my eye, and I see myself through his eyes for a second, all open-mouthed and fish-faced. Still. He's seen me looking worse. Ugly-crying, the works. And Steffan being Steffan, he knows exactly what I'm thinking, too.

"Nobody's perfect, remember? Parents included. His, yours. Mine…"

"But Steff—"

"Nope."

"Steff—"

"Not listening." He's stuffed his fingers in his ears.

"*Steff!*"

Whatever I'm about to say, or however he's about to stop me, it doesn't matter. It doesn't matter because Jared suddenly pushes himself up and leaps out of the boat, sprinting away from us across the beach and into the dark. The little dinghy rocks wildly on the sand – and then Steffan and I are both out of the boat too and chasing him into the night.

Steff, always so much faster than me, streaks ahead in the darkness. I can hear the *ffut ffut ffut* of his feet in the sand, hear it scattering behind him – and it's funny, because this is so very like it was earlier, with the three of us racing across the sand...only this time it's backwards and wrong and I'm still so angry with myself for not seeing it before.

Because it's not about me, is it? It's not about me and it's not about Steffan and it's not about Jared: it's bigger than that. It's about the damage our parents have done in their own way – to each of us, to all of us, to each other. Even when they didn't mean to. It's about the distance we put between them and us; the distance we *need* to put between them and us, just like the distance Jared's trying so hard to put between himself and Steffan right now.

He's running the wrong way. He's running into the dark and away from his friends, deeper and deeper into the shadow his father casts. The *wrong way*.

The bonfire lies far behind us now, and they're somewhere ahead of me, and there I am caught between the two. Always the way. I can just make out their silhouettes, hear their voices – quieter than I'd expected. One of them grabbing at the other, and the other shoving back and lashing out. Lashing out less at his friend and more at the world, at the past, at the sheer unfairness of being his father and mother's son...

But he's more than that, isn't he? We all are.

I've almost reached them when I hear Jared's voice raised. "Don't you think I feel bad enough already? What do you want me to say? That I feel like it's my fault? That you have to move away, that I lose my best mate because of what my dad did? Fine. I've said it. Does that make you happy? Does it make it better?" I see his hand slamming into Steffan's chest, see Steff tumble backwards and land on his back in the sand. Jared leans forward and grabs a handful of his T-shirt, hauling him to his feet – and Steff raises his hands but Jared's not letting go and I'm running faster than I ever thought I could because this is one of those moments when the world shifts and we could spin away and apart... and if we do, what will pull us back together?

"Stop!"

Their heads turn towards me – but Jared's other hand is still raised, and even as he lets go of Steffan's shirt and steps back, he shakes his head and leans in close and says something quiet and low...and now it's Steff's turn to lose his temper. I don't know what Jared said but it's pushed his buttons, and his pride is wounded and he has to Be A Big Man. He puffs his chest out and steps in close to Jared again, his face in Jared's and a finger jabbing at his chest so that Jared is forced to take a step back...and everything is tipping and spinning, and then I've reached them and I'm sliding between them and pushing them apart.

And here we are.

Steffan. Me. Jared.

* * *

226

We define ourselves by our relationships to each other. The Quiet One. The Rich One (well, that's going to have to change, isn't it?). The Responsible One. We define ourselves by our relationships to our parents: what they've done, who *they* are. Who we think they are. We pick our way between the open wounds they've left, but sooner or later every open wound will fester.

Sometimes, you just have to let the wounds close.

"You really want this to be how it ends? Do you?" I look from one to the other of them. To Steffan: "You think this would make your mum proud? You want to take *this* with you to her grave tomorrow? All mouth, no heart. That's not you. Get a grip."

To Jared: "You want to let him win? You want to let your dad take everything you are, everything you *really* have from you too? All that talk, all that stuff about being better? Well, *you're* better than this – and you know it. *I* know it."

Neither of them answers. Smart boys.

"Right then. Let it go. Just…let it go."

On either side of me, they relax. The shadows of their parents, their fathers and their mothers, pass over us and drift away into the night – just like my own mother's will. In time.

"Are we done?" I'm reluctant to drop my hands, in case my palms are the only things keeping them from tearing seven shades of shit out of one another. We all know they could have stepped around me, but it's symbolic, isn't it? And we all know Steffan can't simply stop feeling what he's feeling – and neither can Jared…but now they know what's at stake. They've weighed it and measured it, seen the two ways this could go. And they've both chosen the same direction. There's a long pause and then…

"You know you sound just like Mrs Harris from school, right?" Steffan says it with more than a hint of a snigger.

"*Just* like her," echoes Jared – and if I'm not mistaken, that sounds like he's actually smiling.

That's it. The wound closes and the boat stops rocking and the world is steady again – or as steady as it's going to be – because they are. And here I am, and yet again the joke's on me as I roll my eyes and turn back towards the bonfire and the boat and a terrible hostel bed for the night; here I am and I'm *exhausted*.

Anyway, I always thought Mrs Harris was pretty cool…

"I'm fine…"

I wake with the words still on my tongue. They taste bitter, false. They taste that way because that's what they are, even in the dark.

It was a nightmare – one which has jerked me awake in the small hours with the sheets sticking to me and the hostel's thin pillow scrunched into a ball somewhere beneath my ribcage.

I'm glad I'm alone. The surfer contingent staying here is largely male, which means the women's dorm rooms (handily decorated with pink curtains and door numbers instead of blue because *oh my god, why…?*) are pretty empty – and as a result, I have a four-person pink room all to myself. It overlooks the sea. I can hear the waves through the open window as I swing my legs out of bed and sit up, running my hands through my sweat-dampened hair.

Fragments of my dream come back to me, tumbling past me one by one. There is my father sitting at the kitchen table. There is the key to the front door.

There is my mother's coffin, red roses stark against the lid in the middle of a grey church.

There is my mother, dancing to opera in her bare feet as she cooks. The kitchen window is open. She conducts her imagined orchestra with a spoon.

There is my mother sitting at the kitchen table, a bottle and a glass in front of her.

There is a pile of spoiled sheets; ruined clothing wrapped in plastic.

There is the card the police officer handed me, clutched in my fingers until the edges turned soft.

There is a line of people dressed in black. They open their mouths and their single, shared voice says, "Lovely funeral, lovely funeral", like a parrot.

There is a hole in the earth. A well. A grave. A darkness so complete that there is no way through it, no way back, and I am staring down into it…

And there, across the dark as it gapes at me, as it yawns and threatens to swallow me and everything that I am or ever could be, there is a light. A tiny, single light.

And there is Steffan, picking me up and throwing me into the sea.

There is Steffan, picking me up on the first day we met and setting me back on my feet.

There is Steffan, waiting by the river with beer.

There are my shoes floating away downstream.

There is the water sparkling in the sunshine – and there is Jared, a line of freckles beneath his collarbone as the late summer sun dusts him with gold.

There is Jared, waiting for me outside a changing-block door.

There is Jared.

And there am I: from quite outside myself I see me, climbing up through the sunroof of Steffan's car. I throw my arms out and tip my head back and the sun is on my face…and behind me, the ground gives way and the earth collapses in on itself like a black hole sucking me in – and I wake with the same lie on my lips that I've been telling everyone, telling myself, over and over again. I'm fine.

I am not fine.

I'm not.

But I will be, and that's what matters. Not today, not tomorrow. But sometime. I *will* be fine.

What happens to me doesn't define me.

I am not my mother's drinking, not my mother's death – no more than Steffan is his mother's death or Jared is his father's crimes.

We are not our histories, however deep they cut or however much they scar us.

Whatever guilt we feel, rightly or wrongly, whatever baggage we carry, it is not all that we are.

I did not bury my *self* with my mother.

I am more.

I am me.

Outside the window, the waves wash in and out. Up and down the beach. The sound they make is slow, steady. I force my breaths to match. In and out. In and out. In and out.

I rummage in my bag, pull out jeans and a top; find the flip-flops that are buried at the bottom beneath what looks like a carrier bag full of scrunched-up crisp packets. (I'll be asking Steffan how that got there.)

Locking the door behind me, I make my way along the corridor – feeling along the walls as my eyes adjust to the gloom. I could switch on the hallway lights, I suppose –

there are timer switches all along the walls – but I don't feel like it. The dark suits me for now. The last door before the stairwell is the twin room Steffan and Jared were assigned. I stop in front of it, my fingertips resting lightly on the door. I can feel the grain of the wood, even under the thick paint. Two individual snores seep through from the other side – rising and falling, in and out. Like the sea. I could knock on the door and wake them, but what for?

Instead, I flip-flop my way down the stairs and into the lobby – wedging the entrance door open with a rolled-up magazine. There's a stern sign by the doorway warning that the door is locked at midnight, and you'll need a key card (available at the reception desk for a five pound deposit, refundable on return less a two pound handling charge…) which, needless to say, I don't have. So a rolled-up magazine it is.

Outside, the air is cool; cooler than it's been for weeks. The unexpected chill makes my skin tingle. Everything smells of the sea. Clean and fresh and cool – not muddy like the river, and not baked under the hot sun. The tide is its own thing, moving in and out and wiping away all traces of what was there before it came. There are real waves now, proper waves: no trace of that mirror-stillness remains from the evening. The surfers will be happy. There's a breeze and the faintest suggestion of rain in the air. I can smell it, even though it's still a long way off. Maybe it's a storm coming. Maybe the weather is about to break. Somewhere in the quiet, a church clock chimes three.

I sit in the middle of the slipway, drawing my knees up to my chin and looking out into the black where the sea meets the sky. It's lighter than I thought; there's no moon, but the sky is clear – and over the sea, with no cities and not even a big town nearby, that means there are stars. Thousands of them. Millions. They're scattered across the sky like pebbles on the beach, and the more I look at them the more I see. Stars fill the sky, and suddenly it's not black but a blue velvet cloth spread over the world and covered with diamonds.

"Mum used to look at the stars," says someone behind me. "When she was sick, she used to point up at the sky and say that we didn't matter to the stars, so isn't it funny how much they matter to us." Steffan's voice is still thick with sleep, and I can tell that he's already thinking about his mother's grave, about tomorrow. Today. Later. Whatever. He eases himself down onto the concrete of the slipway. His hair is sticking up in a dozen different directions and he has creases down one side of his face from his pillow. I rest my head on his shoulder and he continues. "Maybe it's not the stars we're looking up at. Not really. Maybe we're looking up, and we're hoping that someone's up there and looking back at us. And not thinking that we're cocking it up."

"Nice. Really philosophical, with the 'cocking it up'."

"I thought so."

We both look out to sea, up at the stars. Up and out and away from everything else and listening to the waves coming and going.

"Steff?"

"Yeah?"

"You did wedge the door open again when you came out, didn't you?"

"Ahhh, crap."

"Thought not."

I don't ask whether Jared is with him. I don't need to; I know he's there without asking. Hanging back and watching, listening. Leaning away from Steffan, I look round – back up the slipway towards the wall. There he is, leaning against the stone as though he was carved from it. The only part of him that moves is his hair, ruffled by the invisible hands of the wind. What would it be like to run my fingers through his hair; to twine them through and wind it between my fingertips, to curl it around and around and to draw him to me? To lean into *him*? What would the stars look like reflected in his eyes – and what does he see when he looks up at them?

"What time do they unlock the front door?" Steffan asks sheepishly.

"I have *no* idea," I say – and even as I say it, I can feel the laugh bubbling up inside me. I can't stop it – couldn't even if I wanted to. It rolls up and out and away like the waves, *in* waves. Because despite it all, despite *everything*, I think I'm happy. Right here, right now, I am content. I feel like I'm on the edge of something; like we *all* are. Like the road, the world, the sky...it's all opening up in front of us, and whether we choose to take it together or we take it alone, it's *ours*.

I wish I could bottle this moment. I wish there was a way that I could consider it for long enough to etch it into my mind for ever – not just as a memory, but as an instant caught in glass. Something tangible that I could hold in my palm, frozen. I could collect them: snow globes full of days, of minutes. Captured and kept to look back at on some far-distant afternoon; something I could pick up and turn over in my hands and smile at as I saw it again, as fresh and as clear and as vivid as it is now. This moment. For no other reason than my being happy.

And the tide moves in and moves out and wipes away all traces of what was there before it came.

**limpet's iPhone / music / playlists / road trip**

Panic! At the Disco - *The Ballad of Mona Lisa*
Beyoncé feat. Jay Z - *Crazy in Love*
Paramore - *Still Into You*
Vienna Teng - *Level Up*
Daft Punk - *Instant Crush*
The Infinite Wilds - *Vow*
Tiger Please - *Without Country*
Frank Turner - *Oh Brother*
Don Henley - *Boys of Summer*
The Script - *If You Could See Me Now*
Fall Out Boy - *Young Volcanoes*


**limpet iPhone / notes & reminders**

Pay back S dinner: cashpoint
Chapel. Flowers for S Mum?
Learn to surf… (kidding)
Earplugs
Wristbands!
Buy S map of USA. He'll need it…

# twenty-two

"I am *so* tired."

"Yeah, well, at least you're not driving later."

"Serves you right. You're the one who forgot to wedge the bloody door open after you."

"And you're the one who goes prancing off down to the beach in the middle of the night, aren't you?"

"At least I made sure I could *get back in*…"

Steffan thinks better of responding to that. Instead, he goes back to chewing. I suspect this is one hostel which is going to regret offering an all-you-can-eat breakfast. There was a massive pile of croissants on the table at the far end of the room until Jared and Steffan got going – and between the two of them, they've just about emptied one tea urn.

They're special, these two.

The plan goes like this: demolish all food stocks in the immediate area, leaving the breakfast buffet a desolate and barren wasteland (in their case, anyway – I'm happy with an orange juice and a bowl of cornflakes, thanks for asking) and then move on. The first place we have to go, of course, is Steffan's mother's grave. It isn't far from here, but he'll want to stay a while – especially if this is his last time. And, after that, it's on to Gethin's band's festival. To my deep and undying joy, there's apparently a camping ground there. Yay.

And this is it. Today. This is really it. Steffan mumbles something about home, and it hits me that this one time – of all times – he meant what he said (however vague it sounded at the time). A couple of days, a few nights. The three of us, one last time. Maybe I thought he'd change his mind; that he'd turn around in the driver's seat and grin and ask what would happen if we just kept driving. But no. Instead, we'll camp at the festival site tonight and then, tomorrow, it's done. Not *us*, but only just.

I think back over last night, how they almost lost each other and how close we came to all splitting apart. Has Steffan had that resentment eating away at his insides all this time? Has it coloured everything, tainted it? I can't believe that, somehow. It's not Steffan, not at all. He wouldn't let something Jared couldn't help ruin their friendship – not now, not ever…but I guess it was just too much. Two days in a little metal box and all this stuff in the air. His mother, my mother. Jared's father. Having to move, having to leave, having to do all these things we can't talk about to one another for fear of hurting the people we love… Well. It would be too much, wouldn't it?

How did he keep going? How did he keep it all inside for so long? How *does* he do it? Because now, it's almost like nothing happened. Almost.

Where does Steffan get his strength from? Did he find it somewhere, or has he had it all along and I've just taken it for granted? Have I got so used to leaning on him that I only see his strength when it snaps for a second?

Where does Jared get *his* from? To walk along carrying all that guilt – guilt that isn't even his – and to still hold his head up high. To look the world in the eye and ask it to take its best shot, because he won't go down without a fight.

How do they do it…and when did the two boys I've grown up with turn into this? Into…*men*, I guess. Ugh.

I don't know, I don't know any of it, but I'm glad it's gone the way it has – because we're still here. Still *us*. And soon we go home. Steffan back to his house to pack, and to say goodbye. Jared back to – presumably – his grandparents. For however long he stays – because that map will never stop calling him.

And me? What do I go back to?

Amy, for now. And after? My father, I guess. And trying to put back together something so broken that I don't even know what it's meant to look like – like trying to glue a broken vase back together in the dark. Where do I even start? But that's a question I'd rather not think about. Not yet, anyway. After all, tomorrow's another day and this one is still fresh and new and – apparently – full of Danish pastries.

Well. It *was*, anyway.

Maybe *that's* how they do it. With the help of baked goods. *Lots* of baked goods.

Behind the buffet table there are big picture windows which look out onto the sea. Already I can see a handful of surfers out on the water, bobbing up and down on their boards.

Jared follows my gaze and cranes his neck around to see what I'm looking at. His nose wrinkles. He's still not keen on surfers – hasn't been since one nearly crashed into him in the sea a few years ago. "What d'you call a group of surfers?" he asks.

Steffan doesn't mind them anywhere near as much as Jared does – after all, he was the one hanging out with them last night. But loyalty is loyalty, so he shrugs. "A toss. A toss of surfers."

He says it a little too loudly, and several bleach-blond-heads snap round to glare at him. I shush him, but to his credit, it *was* pretty funny.

"A toss of surfers," says Jared thoughtfully, folding the last piece of a croissant over on itself and eating it. "Works for me."

They've done all the damage they can do at this particular breakfast stand and it's time to get going. Jared pushes his chair back from the table with a squeal, metal legs scraping across the plastic floor. Thanks to Steffan's total inability to keep his enormous mouth shut, *everyone* in the room is now watching us. Which is excellent. Someone at the surfiest-looking table mutters something as we pass, and the rest of the group sniggers – but this doesn't bother Jared one bit. Instead, he manages to knock into every single one of their chairs as he passes. One of the surfers spills a mug of coffee all over the table (and, crucially, his breakfast). He jumps up, hot liquid dripping from his artfully-distressed shirt.

"Oops," says Jared. "Didn't see you there."

"Stop it," I hiss, nudging him in the ribs – and he jerks back as though he's been stung. I'm sure that's a pout. Jared's pouting. Honestly.

That little hiccup over and done with, I stride out of the dining room and promptly trip over a chair in the lobby. Because that's the kind of thing that happens to me, isn't it? I attract this sort of stuff. Moral high ground...followed by falling over. It's probably karma or something. Not that I'm much of a believer in that lately.

I run up the stairs and grab my bag from the room, doing my best to straighten the bedding before pulling the door shut behind me. By the time I've made it to the car, the two

241

of them are already out there: Jared putting his rucksack into the boot and Steffan doing something with his violin. I think he's talking to it.

"Steff…" I hold up the bag of rubbish I found and raise my eyebrows at him expectantly. "You want to explain how this happened to find its way into my bag?"

"That? Well. Now." He sets the violin back in its case and closes the latches carefully. "It must've just fallen in, in the back."

"You mean like my bag just fell open, all by itself?"

"That. Yes."

"Steffan?"

"Yes." He's dropped his chin down to his chest and looks like a puppy. I'm scolding a puppy. What kind of a monster am I?

Yeah, I'm not falling for that one.

"Don't ever go into a girl's bag, and especially not mine. It's more than your life's worth." I hand him the rubbish bag.

"Why? What's hiding in there? Something we menfolk aren't meant to see?"

"Socks, mostly. And as for the 'menfolk' thing? I'm going to pretend I didn't hear that." I wink at him.

"Careful. I might have you taken off the guest list…" He wags a finger at me, and I stick my tongue out at him.

"You mean at your big gig? Wow. You've *changed*, man.

Oh, how you've changed." I place my hand over my heart and shake my head in mock-sadness. He flicks his middle finger up at me.

Jared has stood back and is taking all this in with his usual half-amused smile. Just as he always does. I realize with a pang of something like regret that this is what I will miss the most: the *ease* of being around Steffan. I can't imagine how it will be without him here, without this. Without one or other of us slinging insults at him and him slinging them straight back again.

What are we without Steffan? Will we be the same, or will we be different? Will *this* – whatever it is, because I thought I knew but now I realize I didn't – will this evaporate like a vapour trail when he leaves, or will it remain? Will there be anything more than an echo; the ghosts of the three of us forever running up and down the beach?

Time ticks past and the stars look down on us and the waves move in and out, and what is it all for?

Moments, suspended in snow globes. That's what it's for.


Having made a big fuss about being ready to go, once the bags are in the car, Steffan loses all his enthusiasm.

Part of him wants to go and get ready for his big rock

star moment (even though at this time of day, he's mostly going to find an empty field – and I know Steffan well enough to know that he wants to Make An Entrance) but before that, there's the other thing. The graveyard. It's a solemn enough thought to take the shine off his festival plans, even if we all knew it was coming. Both inland from here, on the same road: the graveyard halfway between the beach and the festival site. It's almost like it's fate. He has to go through one to get to the other.

He's dreading it, I think, but he also wants it to be done. To be over. A bit like when you're sitting an exam and there's weeks and weeks before it, but you get to the point where you just wish it would hurry up and be over so you can get on with the rest of your life. You see, until he says goodbye, he can't really move on. The fact his mother can't say goodbye back doesn't make any difference.

I get that. Of all people, I get it. If I'm honest, I was worried about it, when he said he wanted to go and see her – and it's selfish, but I was worried about me more than him… No, that's not quite right. I guess I was worried that I would dissolve into tears or something, leaving him with this soggy, weeping creature to deal with, when what he really wanted – what he *needed* – was to get some closure. I couldn't let him do it without me, either: that's not how we work, is it? But, oh. The pressure.

What I don't really get, on the other hand, is why this

whole festival thing is such a big deal to him. He's played in concerts before. He's performed at complicated things that have been on television and everything. This will just be a bunch of the kids from school, and the kids like us from every other school for miles around, drinking warm cider and pretending it's just the same as Glastonbury.

Maybe *that's* why it's so important: because it's *here*, in our little corner of the world, the place where we've all grown up together. It's all part of the same thing: his goodbye. His swansong. Just like this whole trip – all his idea, casually tossed into the conversation like it didn't matter. The driving, the camping, the visit to the grave: it's his way of shutting up shop, pulling down the blinds. The Steffan Show will give one last performance and then the circus moves on.

And what about the people he leaves behind?

Will *he* miss *us*?

I sit cross-legged on the wall opposite the pub while they fiddle with the car radiator – and as I do, a woman walks past me. She doesn't stop, doesn't even give any sign she's noticed I'm there. But I notice her. I notice her because of her shoes.

I know those shoes...or a pair just like them.

Blue suede flat shoes. Nothing special. Just pale blue shoes you shouldn't wear in the rain.

I remember the inside of the shoe shop; the smell of all

245

the new shoes. The feel of the carpet squishing beneath my toes as I put my trainers back on and my mother turned away from the racks of school shoes and pointed at another shelf.

"Look at those!" You'd have thought it was Christmas by the way she sounded.

I remember her trying them on, putting her shopping bag on the floor. I remember the way she sat on the little shoe-shop stool and held both her feet out in front of her; my mother, who I thought believed in sensible shoes above all things.

"They're alright," I said. Sullen. Bored. I wanted to go home. "When are you going to wear them, anyway?"

"I don't know. Maybe I'll save them for somewhere exciting?" She considered her feet again. "You know what? I don't care if I don't wear them. They make me smile. I can just…get them out of the cupboard and look at them from time to time, can't I?"

And I remember the look in her eyes as she said it – and how, for only a second, I saw someone else smiling out from behind them.

*"You aren't the only one looking out at the world, you know."*

But I didn't, did I? I didn't know. And now I'll never have the chance to know who that person who loved the pale blue shoes was. What else did she love that I'll never know about?

Those blue suede shoes.

The last time I saw them, Amy and I were handing them to the undertaker along with the clothes she was to be buried in.

They'd never even been worn once.

The woman walks on, and I spin round to look down to the sea. The surfers are having what I assume counts as an amazing time, falling off their boards. I don't understand. I mean, what's so great about falling over? Even if you are falling into water, you're still falling over. Again and again and again. And then you have to get back up and get back on the board and wait for the next time you fall over. It looks like hard work. I say as much out loud, to nobody in particular.

Of course Jared hears me – well, he would, wouldn't he? Nothing gets past him. I can suddenly *feel* him standing behind me, looking over me to the sea, and I find that I'm almost waiting for his hand on my shoulder, on the small of my back. Something. Anything. Because he's standing so close and yet he feels so distant and I can't even begin to puzzle him out. Is he my friend? Is he something else? Are he and I simply in orbit around Steffan's star – and when Steffan goes, will he go too, drifting off into the dark?

I never used to be afraid of the dark.

"You're thinking about Steffan." It isn't a question.

"I don't want him to go," I say, and my voice sounds

tight. Weak. "I don't know what I'm going to do without him around."

"Don't let him hear you saying that. He's already bad enough this morning with this festival shit happening. Imagine what he'd be like if he heard you!"

"He'd never get his head in the car..." I shake my own head, and turn to face him, looking up as he stands over me. "What about you?"

"What about me?"

I wait for the shutters to come down behind his eyes, for the distance between us to grow as he steps back from the question. But he doesn't. Instead, he sighs. His forehead creases a little. I wait.

"I'll be fine. It's just life, isn't it? You keep your head down and you just... I don't suppose rugby...?"

"No sports analogies. Because, *sport*."

"Fine." His frown vanishes and he smiles down at me, his eyes locking onto mine. "You put your head down and you run."

"No sport."

"That wasn't sport. That was life!"

"Then you may continue." I tear my gaze away from his. I can't hold it any longer: there's so much in his look. Too much. He's as afraid as I am, and I can see it. He's letting me see it because he can't say it out loud. The walls that he's built around himself, the ones he built as protection, they're

248

pinning him in. And while he's locked out at least some of the bad, some of the pain, there are other things he's locked out too. The good things.

High walls and small windows may keep enemies out, but they'll keep friends out too. You build yourself a fortress to keep you safe and you retreat inside it and, before you know it, you've made your very own prison and thrown away the key.

Which one of us is right? Jared, who decided that no one was going to hurt him again? Or me, who tries to let everything in and ends up missing the things that matter? Or are we both as wrong as each other?

What will he do, now that his dad's back? The rumours and the talk will pick up and follow him round like litter caught in the wind. Everywhere he goes, there will be whispers, and I already know how that makes him feel. Words like arrows aimed for his heart. His walls are too high now to be breached – but every well-chosen missile will leave a mark.

He hasn't spoken again.

"Are you going to stay at your grandparents' when he comes back?" Of course, this is the catch. Jared might trust them, might even be happy to live with them...but so is his dad. When he's not in jail, that is.

He scrunches up his nose. "I don't know. I don't want to. I don't like him and I don't trust him. But…" He tails off.

*But.* Exactly. That wasn't there before, was it?

"What about your mum?"

"She's got a new family now. I hope they make her happy."

"Wow."

"I want her to be happy, you know? I really do. I just...I just wish that being my mum didn't make her so *un*happy."

How do you follow that? What do you say? What can make that feel better? My mother's dead; she doesn't have opinions any more. She can't do anything, say anything. I'm free to think what I want about her, and to construct my own versions of what she thought of me.

Jared doesn't get to do that. His mother has made it abundantly clear what she thinks of him. No wonder he imagines what his life would be like if he could change places with either me or Steff.

I do the only thing I can. I reach out to take hold of his hand...

"Figure we might as well go anyway..." Steffan slams the bonnet shut and strolls towards us, and I drop my hand. My fingertips ache from the need to touch Jared; my blood throbs beneath my skin.

The wind catches my hair, whipping it round into my face, and as I turn my head to brush it away I see Steff pause. There's a hitch in his step – as though he's afraid he's interrupting something but has realized too late and now he's committed. I feel Jared move back.

Whatever there was between us then, at that moment, it slips away. No snow globes here.

Steffan carries on. "Gethin reckons…"

And on…and on…and on… Gethin this, Gethin that. Bloody *Gethin*. Behind his back, Jared is making heart shapes with his thumbs and forefingers every time Steffan says "Gethin". Sometimes, he doesn't even have time to pull his hands apart from the last gesture before he has to make the next one. And every single time, he bats his eyelashes and puts on a dreamy face.

I start coughing.

Steffan stops talking, looks at me suspiciously and then whips round to glare at Jared. Jared flutters his eyelashes at him, blows him a kiss and collapses into laughter.

Steff looks wounded. Jared elbows him as he slips past and wanders off down the wall towards the slipway, patting down his pockets as though he's looking for something.

"Heard from your aunt?" Steffan's watching me watching Jared.

"I need to text her and let her know I'll be back tomorrow." The thought of going home fills me with a dull ache. Here, I am through the looking glass. Here, everything makes sense.

"How's stuff at home?"

"I don't know. I mean, I *do* know, but I don't know if it's home any more; if it'll *feel* like home. You know?"

"I basically don't *know* anything. Especially not what that question meant."

"You're so annoying."

"It's why you love me."

"'Love' is such a strong word, don't you think? I'd go with something more along the lines of 'tolerate'."

"Alright, then. It's why you tolerate me." He winks at me.

"Dad's gone into treatment."

"You mean rehab? Thank Christ for that. It couldn't go on. *You* couldn't go on with it like that."

"He didn't want to go."

"I bet he didn't. I bet he was happy just to leave you to deal with all the shit that needs doing."

"Don't, Steff."

"You listen to me. Your father's selfish. Mine might be a bloody long way off perfect —" he rolls his eyes — "but when Mum died he was there, and *he took care of me.* You had to plan a funeral, Lim. *You* had to do that. That shouldn't be."

I turn away, and he ducks back into my field of vision. "No. You need to hear this, and if nobody else will tell you, then I *will*. He's a selfish bastard and he's put all this on you—" His eyes widen at my expression and he draws his head back. "And shit on a stick, he's made you feel like it's your fault, hasn't he?"

I didn't move fast enough, did I?

I dropped my guard, I slowed down.

And Steffan…Steffan, of all people, has seen.

His voice when he speaks again is soft but somehow hard at the same time – and when I meet his eyes they are fiery with anger. Not at me, I think, but at the perceived injustice he's discovered. He's angry *for* me.

"You are not responsible for your mother, Lim. Not the way she lived, not the way she died. Not one bit. And if your father – your *father* – is letting you think otherwise, then he doesn't deserve to call you family."

"It's not that easy…"

"It really is, you know. Your mother. Not your fault. See? *Easy*." He drops into a crouch in front of me and grabs both my hands, closing his around them. "Don't you dare let anyone tell you any different. Least of all him. He needs to handle his own bullshit. Don't let him try and offload it onto you."

I sniff.

I am not going to let this win. This sadness, this guilt. This everything, which threatens to drag me back down into the dark every time I think I've buried it.

Grief is unpredictable, they said; everyone feels it differently. They made it sound like a piece of art: an abstract painting that everybody sees something different in, something unique to them.

Grief – my grief – is an animal. It stalks me and I set traps to catch it: traps to cage it and shatter it and starve it of air. I want to see it wither away to nothing, until it's less than a memory, less than a ghost. But it has claws and it has teeth and they are deep in me – and the worst of it is that sometimes, sometimes I forget. I'm so used to the barbs that I forget that they're there, and every time I forget I think I can move on – and then suddenly, I remember. And each time I remember it's like someone has reached into my body and torn out my insides all over again. Because, you see, I know everything that Steffan tells me is true – of course I do. And this grief, this animal, this *thing*… it isn't just for my mother. I lost more than my mother that night. My father is still here, but somehow he's not – not quite. He isn't who I thought he was, and it took all this for either of us to know it. At least we have *that* in common…

When she stopped, everything stopped – and more than her, that's what I'm mourning.

Maybe I'm wrong. Maybe it's not an animal after all. Maybe my grief is a parasite.

It will not bleed me dry.

I won't let it.

Steffan's smiling at me.

"There it is," he says. He squeezes my hands.

"There what is?"

"The moment when you told all the bad, all the shit, *all* of it, to go to hell because you don't want it any more. I remember it." He grins.

Maybe, just maybe, he does understand after all.

# twenty-three

Steffan makes a point of not driving past the ostrich farm again. I think one stare-down with an angry bird was probably enough for him – and I'm still not sure who actually won. If you pushed me, I'd probably give it to the ostrich. It scares me more than Steffan does.

Instead, he takes the winding road back inland, which is, apparently, being used by every caravan in the western hemisphere. And a lot of tractors. And some hay lorries. Just because.

We don't go anywhere fast.

The road meanders through fields and along the sides of hills. There are steep rocks on one side, and on the other a sharp drop to an old railway line – the sleepers long since pilfered to mark out beds for vegetable gardens – and the beginnings of a river. It sparkles in the shifting light. A quarry cut into the hillside has a thick, rusty chain wrapped through its wire gates. Someone's spray-painted *JESUS SAVES* in big red letters on the rock. Someone else has painted *DON'T TRUST THE BANKS* in thick black letters underneath it. Yet another person has drawn a huge white flower through both of them. I'm not even going to try and figure out what that's supposed to mean.

The further we follow the road, the thicker the trees become; the more they overhang and box us in. Even with the little row of caravans tootling along in front of us, it's spooky – like driving deeper and deeper into an enchanted forest. Steffan pushes his sunglasses up onto his head as the darkness thickens.

The canopy of the trees has formed a tunnel; cut through by the traffic, the branches arch over the road and turn everything green. Even the air coming in through the windows smells green: damp and mossy. It's like being in the middle of a huge leafy cathedral. Spokes of golden-white light punch through the greenery – so thick and bright that I could almost reach out and take hold of one. Dust motes dance up and down them.

I don't even mind our being stuck behind the caravans; anything to make this last a little longer. I could stay here for ever. It's cool and calm and so peaceful. It's beautiful. Nothing can touch me in here.

And then, without warning, the canopy drops back and away, and we're in a car and on the road to the chapel, chugging along behind a bunch of sunburned holidaymakers and what looks like *all* their worldly goods, snail-like in their caravans.

It's Jared who spots the bikes. All neatly parked up on the grass verge, with fading cow parsley and nettles spilling out of the hedgerow over them. And they're not just any motorbikes; these are the real deal – the big cruising bikes that thunder up and down the American highways of Jared's imagination. Of *course* it's Jared who spots them.

Dozens and dozens of them, all lined up; their riders' helmets beside them or balanced on their seats.

"Uhhhh…" Steffan makes a noise.

"Must be a thing," says Jared. I can see him looking around.

"It's the dual carriageway, isn't it?" says Steffan – and with his usual carefree attitude to road safety, he swings the car straight across the road and pulls up on the opposite verge.

He's right. Up ahead, on the bridge where this tiny little country road crosses the dual carriageway (the one all those caravan drivers *should* be on, according to Steff, so they don't clutter up the blah-blah-blah boring…) there's a little crowd.

A surprisingly large crowd, come to think of it.

It lines both sides of the bridge, pressed up against the railings. It's dressed in black leather, in jeans, in T-shirts, in jackets…

It's all the bikes' owners.

They're waiting for something.

For Steffan, it's the most natural thing in the world to walk up to a massive crowd of bikers and ask them how it's going. Jared wanders up after him, his fingers turning his lighter over and over and over.

I hang back. I'm not as much a fan of people. Not really. I mean, they're fine; I just don't always want to be around them so much. They're hard work. Tiring.

Steffan's chatting away and they're pointing down at the carriageway and nodding – and he laughs. They nod some more. He gestures along the bridge. Several of the bikers look round. They're looking at me. Steffan waves me over.

"You'll like this," he says, and he shoves a puffy envelope into my hand, shuffling me towards the railing. Two enormous bikers – one with a beard the size of a small dog – edge sideways to make a gap. Steff manoeuvres me into it. "These guys are all from the same bike club, right? And two of their friends just got married and they're leaving for their honeymoon."

"That's…nice."

There's probably a point. I'm just not quite there yet.

"They're coming this way on their bikes. In convoy with

the rest of the club. So this lot have come on ahead to wait for them…" He waves his envelope at me, opening the flap and pinching out a load of white and pink tissue paper cut into shapes. I see bells and horseshoes and other wedding-related things.

Ah. Confetti. Got it. Told you I'd get there.

It doesn't take long; I've barely even slotted into my (tiny) gap between two vast leather shoulders – Beard Man on my right, Tassel Jacket Man on my left – while Steffan and Jared have found gaps further up and down the line, when someone says, "Here they come!"

We hear them before we see them. It's a loud, low, gurgling roar that builds and builds. It's like thunder, only more…engine-y. A lot more engine-y. They're moving slowly, side by side. They even have a police outrider escorting them as they head up the carriageway. The chrome sparkles in the sunshine and several of the bikes are decked out with white ribbons that flutter in the slipstream. As they come closer, everyone on the bridge starts to cheer and clap – and then the clapping stops and everyone starts emptying the confetti-filled envelopes.

As it falls, the confetti looks like it's dancing. Pink hearts and white stars are caught on the breeze. They rise and fall as we lean over the railing and throw them by the handful. The bikes passing beneath us – already deafening – sound their horns. The riders wave up at us and we wave back at them and everybody's cheering and laughing. Down the line, Steffan is upending his envelope of confetti; he shakes it to make sure every last scrap is out. Up the line, Jared is watching the bikes. I can see him through the cloud of little paper shapes as they tumble and spin.

The last of the convoy passes underneath to a final cheer – and suddenly our new friends are all hurrying for their bikes, pulling on helmets and kicking their stands away as the engines start. Big Beard Man pats Steffan on the shoulder as he walks back to his bike and yanks his helmet back on.

One by one, the bikes pull out onto the lane and roar off towards the next village and the slip road onto the carriageway to join the rest of the convoy.

The last of them pulls away with a blast of his horn as we walk back to the Rust Bucket – and as Steffan holds the door open for me to clamber in, he picks a bit of confetti out of my hair. A crumpled heart flutters to the ground.

# twenty-four

Steffan turns the key and switches off the ignition. The car's engine stops and we sit in silence. His fingers stay on the steering wheel, holding on to it like it's a lifebelt.

"You don't have to come," he says after a long pause.

Jared blinks at him and shakes his head.

In the back, I unclip my seat belt. "You're kidding, right?"

"No, funnily enough." He swivels in his seat, turning to look back at me. "I'm not. It's not like it's a big deal, not now. And you've…" He stops, bites his lip and frowns. He's trying to figure out the right way to say it, whatever *it* is. Eventually, he hits on something he thinks will work. "I can't ask you—"

"That's just it, you idiot," I say, cutting him off. "You never *have* to ask. Now shift your arse so I can get out of the car, would you?"

He looks at me for a moment longer; long enough for me to see something that might be gratitude in his eyes.

*Maybe.*


Unlike my mother's grave, fresh and cold and double-deep in the cemetery on the edge of town, Steffan's mother is buried beside the chapel in the village where she was born. It's high on a hill, and in one direction you can see the fields laid out like a cloth. In the other, the sea shines silver in the distance. Come the winter, the air smells of woodsmoke from all the open fires in the village, and everyone huddles around the hearth in the pub with their pints. Now, in the summer, it smells of the honeysuckle in the hedges, of the pollen rising from the fields, of the jasmine that Steffan planted beside his mother's headstone.

I was with him when he did it, all the while quietly talking in Welsh to someone who could no longer hear him. His dad, not quite understanding why he needed – not just wanted, but *needed* – to do it, paced the boundary of the little graveyard. I understood back then, because Steff was my friend. I understand now because I've seen how very deep a freshly-dug grave becomes the second your mother's coffin is lowered into it. He simply couldn't bear the thought of his mother, who loved flowers and baking, of this person so full of life, lying alone in the ground. He couldn't stand the idea of the only flowers she ever got being a bunch of petrol-station carnations wrapped in noisy cellophane, left to rot and shrivel to nothing and adding death to death. So he bought a jasmine plant from the florist in town and he dug a little hole at the side of her headstone and he planted it.

And then we dug it back out again because he'd planted it still in its pot, and it only occurred to us *after* he'd finished that that probably wasn't the way to go. She'd have laughed at that.

For all the views and the honeysuckle and the jasmine, though, the chapel is just the same as I remember it: cold and grey and all hard edges. That's chapel for you. Even in the sunshine it looks forbidding. I never got how someone like Steffan's mother could possibly think she belonged in front of a building like this: one which permanently looks like it's about to tell you off for eating a biscuit, because biscuit equals joy equals bad... Bad biscuit. Bad happy. Bad, bad, bad. But that's what she wanted. It's what she chose, after all. She wanted to go back to where she came from – and I guess we've all got to come from somewhere.

What will we do when it's our turn? I wonder. Will we want to look forward, or back?

Jared lurks by the graveyard wall, pretending to read an inscription. Steffan folds himself into a rugby player-shaped heap beside the headstone, picking the faded flowers off the jasmine and curling his fingers tightly around them. The lettering on the stone has started to weather already, her name softening. It's what happens, isn't it? Memories soften, stones weather. Names – so important to us when we're using them – fill up with moss. Time passes and we can never go back, not really – only forward. Forward, and making the best of it as we go.

I hang back from the graveside. He needs some space, and I need to be not-standing-right-next-to-a-grave-again. Not yet. I'm here if he needs me, which he won't.

The next headstone along has a photo set into it. It's black and white; a woman in an old-fashioned lace wedding dress. Her hair is dark, tightly curled about her face, and she's clutching a bouquet of flowers. She's smiling. Of course she is; it's her wedding day and, looking at all the dates on the stone, she has a good sixty years ahead of her. Sixty years in which she'll see her children grow up to have children of their own…and then for those children to have children too.

My mother didn't get that. Neither did Steffan's. But seeing him sitting there, jabbering away in Welsh and clutching a handful of jasmine flowers…I don't know, it seems kind of crazy being angry about it, doesn't it? What good does it do? It's not fair, and it's not fair…and so it goes. Only forward, never back.

I watch him for a few minutes and when he stops talking

and bows his head, I don't want to give him space any more. Without a word, I sit beside him and put my arm around him. He rests his head on my shoulder and he's not quite crying but it's near enough.

Some goodbyes are harder than others, and the hardest are never quite the ones you expect.

"She'd understand, you know," I say after a while.

"I know." He sits up, rubbing his hand across his face. He sniffs, just once. "That's the worst part. She always did."

"And you feel bad why? For leaving her?"

"Kind of. Stupid, isn't it? I mean, she left me first, right?"

"It's not stupid. It is what it is." I am, momentarily, overwhelmed by my own Zen. Because that's *deep*.

"It is what it is?" He looks at me, mimicking my tone. Apparently Steffan isn't much into Zen.

"Yeah, alright. I thought you were being all mournful and sensitive? I liked that better."

"I'll bet you did…" He nudges me and winks.

"Oh, get over yourself. Seriously."

"Mournful and mysterious. Sensitive. Quiet. That's your type, right?" Another nudge. The bastard.

"Seriously. I'm trying to be nice here. Shut the hell up."

"Whatever." He holds his hands up, still grinning.

The quiet Steffan, the one only his dead mother and I get to see, has vanished again. And that's the way it should be.

Whatever it was he needed to say to her, he's said it – and it's like a weight has lifted from him. Maybe he told her about Jared, about the money. Maybe he told her why they're leaving, and how he's tried so hard to suck it up and not show how much it hurts – and how it spilled out anyway and threatened the thing that matters most to him, because however much he wants to protect the people around him, he's only human. Just like us. Maybe that's what he said. Maybe not. But whatever it was, it's helped. She's helped. Of course she has, because that's what mothers are there for…even when they aren't there any more.

Now all he has to do is figure out where he goes from here.

He's not the only one.


"I do…not…need…a map." Steffan's absolutely adamant about that as we bounce along yet another tiny little road, which will almost inevitably end up with us having to do a complicated U-turn in the yard of yet another farm.

"You have no idea where we are, though, do you?" Many more potholes like that last one and I may well end up being bounced out of the back seat and into their laps in the front. Jared is rummaging in the glovebox for anything resembling a map. What he's found is a load of old chewing gum wrappers and a packet of what used to be jelly babies, all fused together in the heat. He throws the packet back at me. More out of curiosity than anything else, I peel the plastic back off the multicoloured lump – it's kind of disturbing. All the little figures have softened and slumped into one another, the colours blurring where they join, but some of the shapes are still there. A green baby's head is sticking out of an orange one's stomach, and I'm not even going to think about what the pink one's doing...

"I have a brilliant sense of direction, thank you," Steffan mutters as he shuffles forward in his seat and peers at the windscreen.

What he's actually doing, you see, is looking at his phone on the dashboard. He's looking at his phone on the dashboard and hoping against all hope that his GPS will suddenly start working again and he won't have to admit that he was following his satnav all this time and that the app's just crashed.

Sense of direction, my arse.

The best part of it, of course, is that Jared and I both know exactly what he's doing – but it's much more fun to pretend that we don't, and see how he gets himself out of it.

At last, he slams on the brakes and my seat belt yanks me back into my seat.

"Ouch."

"Sorry, sorry." He taps the screen of his phone. "Why can't you see the satellite, then?" He's talking to his phone. Not *on* his phone, *to* his phone. "It'll be in the sky, won't it? Look!" He jabs a finger at the windscreen. "There's the sky. I can see it, so why can't you, you piece of—"

"Do you two want some time alone?" Jared asks. He's given up on looking for a map – not that there's likely to be anything as useful as that in here anyway. As we've already established, Steffan's car is very like Steffan's head: untidy, full of crap and pretty filthy.

Steff just glares at him. "I'm stepping outside. I may be some time." He grabs his phone (which is probably still full of seawater – no wonder it's being iffy) and shoves the door open, swearing the whole while.

Jared swivels in his seat to look at me. "You getting out?"

"Might as well. He's blatantly got no idea where we are."

"I do, though." There's the tiniest hint of smugness in his voice.

"Seriously? And you're not going to tell him?"

"It's more fun this way. Besides, think how proud he'll be when he figures it out for himself."

"You mean when his phone wakes up."

"That too."

Steffan is pacing up and down outside the car, alternately holding his phone up to the sky and shaking it.

"This is going to take a while, isn't it?" I trace my finger along the inside of the window. It feels slightly greasy, and I wonder what Steffan plans to do with the car when he leaves.

The day he bought it, he drove it round to my house and parked it outside, leaning on the horn until I came out to look at it. It sounded like a wheezy old goat and it looked like shit (and it still does – both of those) but he was so pleased as he stood there with one hand on the roof, smiling and saying "Right?" that you'd think he had actually built it himself. He *did* buy it himself, with his own money saved from those summer jobs his mum made him take (and the infamous stint as the local paper boy...) so maybe that was it. It was his car. Nobody else's.

The thing about the Rust Bucket, though, is that it didn't matter how it looked. It was – *is* – more than just a car. It was freedom. It meant no more waiting around for the bus to school. It meant no more sitting in somebody's room on a Saturday afternoon because it's raining and there's nothing to do and nowhere to go. It meant being able to go places and do things...to do *this*. This, this last thing with the three of us.

Who will take our places in Steffan's new life? Who will sit in Jared's seat? Who will sit in mine? Will they have the same in-jokes or new ones? Will we simply be replaced...?

I feel unkind thinking it, but I can't help myself. Everything is in flux. Everything is changing. The rocks that I stood on are nothing more than sand, washing away beneath my feet. What's underneath that? I wonder. *Is* there anything, or is there simply nothing? A yawning black hole. A grave.

Do we replace people? Not knowingly, perhaps, but do we look for someone – something – to fill a space that has opened up in us? And what does that mean for me? Whose place am I looking to fill?

I know, right? Where would I even begin...?

Jared unfolds himself from the front passenger seat, yawning and stretching as he opens his door and swings his legs out. Steffan is now jabbing at his phone. I have no idea whether there's any practical purpose to it, but it seems to be making him feel better at least; he's pacing less. Jared leans against the side of the car, his hands in his pockets.

Well, fine. It's too hot in here anyway.

I follow them out.

We have wound up on the highest hill for miles. All around us, the countryside drops away into a patchwork of sun-scorched browns and yellows, of green hedges and black specks that, up close, would be cows. There are clouds now – almost unfamiliar after endless days of searing blue heat – and their shadows slide across the valley below us. Tiny cars no bigger than toys wind along roads very like the ones we've been on the last couple of days. Who is in them, I wonder, and where are they going? Are they going to the beach? To the river? To the supermarket? To a festival or a funeral, or all of the above?

On the opposite side of the valley there's a farm, perched on the side of the hill. Built of stone and surrounded by barns, the house looks small and delicate. Fragile, somehow, against the sprawl of the fields and the weight of the other buildings.

And there, on the top of the hill behind it, is something that looks distinctly like a festival tent.

"Steff?"

He doesn't listen. He's progressed to standing in front of the car and pressing random combinations of things on his phone while swearing.

"Steffan?"

"One sec. I've almost—"

"Steffan. *Look*." I march over and stand behind him, putting my hands on his arms and forcibly turning him to face the right direction. "That's where we're meant to be, right?"

"Oh?" He squints at the hill. "Oh. Right."

"Shall we?"

Right on time, his phone chirps. Guess who's just found the satellite?

# twenty-five

A metal fence has been set up all around the festival site. It's not exactly going to keep out your hardened fence-jumper (there's a gap wide enough for me to lie down in right in front of us, for starters) but that's not really the point, is it? It's a token fence. It's more about the *idea* of a fence than the actual fence. It's *essence* of fence.

The guy on the gate is wearing a hi-vis vest and earphones. The earphones upset Steffan, as he's been looking forward to using his "I'm with the band" line the whole way here. Bless. Instead, earphone guy looks at the car, decides we're obviously involved in setting up, sniffs, and waves us through.

You can tell we don't get a whole lot of festivals round here, can't you?

There's a rattly, grindy sort of sound as the bottom of the car scrapes along the dry rut left by a tractor when the ground was wet. After the hot summer, it's hardened to something like concrete and I can almost feel Steffan wince at the drawn-out gouging sound.

We grind to a halt in front of a post with brightly-coloured cardboard arrows cable-tied to it. They're all pointing in different directions; a riot of orange and pink. They're all also written by someone who was both drunk and wearing a blindfold at the time and I can't make out a single word.

Steffan drums his thumbs on the steering wheel thoughtfully. "That look like it could say 'park' to you?"

"As in car park?" Jared leans forward in his seat.

"As in 'buggered if I know'."

"Worth a go, isn't it?"

We follow the arrow.

Two minutes later, we're bumping back the way we came. The sign which Steffan thought said "park" actually said "portaloos". Not the same thing at *all*.

Taking the path of least resistance (which we kind of need to do, because this rut is just getting deeper and deeper), Steffan goes straight past the pointless direction post and dead ahead. I think he's working on the principle that eventually we'll either run out of field or someone will stop us and tell us where to go. Failing that, I wouldn't be surprised if he just parks anywhere.

"Tents!" I can see tents. Camping tents, as opposed to

festival tents. (Steffan, naturally, has already spotted the bar tent. Of course he has.) "There!"

The car lurches in the direction of the camping field. Spotting the narrow gateway that leads into it, Steffan looks at me in the rear-view.

"Want to drive, Lim?"

"That's just mean."

"No sense of humour."

I pull a face at him in the mirror.

This time, I help them with the tents. And when I say "help", I mean "supervise". And when I say "supervise", I mean "stand there holding bits until they want them". Things go smoothly. I am absolutely convinced this is down to my presence.

We leave the bags locked in the car and Steffan sets about trying to find Gethin's camper van. Apparently, it's bright orange with stickers designed to look like bullet holes all down one side. Classy. Mind you, it would still be easy to find even if we didn't know that: it's parked right against the fence at the far side of the camping field, with the doors open and terrible, terrible drum and bass booming out of it. The speakers have been turned up so high that every bass note distorts and squeaks.

Steffan shakes his head sadly. "No one should do that to a stereo."

"Gethin for you." Jared shrugs.

Gethin himself is pacing up and down outside the camper, muttering into the phone clamped to his ear. He nods hello to Steffan and Jared, and does a double take at me, smirking slightly.

Ah.

It would appear that Becca's been talking. Well, that's not exactly a surprise, is it?

Gethin grumbles into his phone one more time and then tosses it into the camper.

"Steff!" He holds out a hand. Steffan looks at it. Gethin drops his hand.

The thing about Gethin is, basically, he's a bit of a dick. Harmless, but still. Dick.

"How's it going, mate?" he says.

He also calls everyone "mate". All the time.

Like I said: *dick*.

Steffan shrugs and mutters something about rehearsal. Gethin smirks and shakes his head. This is not the correct response. Steffan takes a step back. Gethin frowns; raises his hands placatingly.

Jared and I exchange glances. It's like that.

"I think I left my... Need to...not be here. Car." I whisper over Steffan's shoulder. Without taking his eyes off Gethin, he hands me the keys.

Jared falls back slightly, but he doesn't come with me.

276

*Home 2morrow. At music thing – Steff playing. Call u when we're on the way xxx*

I send the text to Amy, and I think how strange this must be for her. How hard. She's just lost her sister, and now here she is, taking care of us all. Even my father, picking him up and trying to put him back together. I can't run away and expect her to pick up the pieces. *That's* not fair. But how can you even start to help someone you barely know? And that's what I've realized: I have no idea who he is any more. I haven't for a long time. But there's two sides to that coin. And maybe it's something we can fix. Maybe not, but it's worth trying, right?

And Amy, poor Amy. Who's taking care of *her*? Someone should take care of her too.

My fingers move over the letters on my phone.

*Hope u'r doing ok? xxx*

It's pathetic, really, isn't it? That that's the best I can do? I mean…yeah. It is. But it's a start.


The spat between Steffan and Gethin has been settled. Gethin has – grudgingly – agreed to rehearse at least one of the songs (having not taken kindly to phrases like "amateur hour" and Steffan's firmly-worded version of "I do not 'wing it', thank you *very* much...") and now there are wristbands. Shiny plastic wristbands in the same neon shades as the indecipherable signposts. Steffan's is bright green, stamped with the letters *VIP* in thick black ink.

There'll be no living with him now.

He beams at me. "VIP, baby."

"Yeah, alright. You're special. *Special.*" I make air-quotes around the word with my fingers.

He snorts and fastens the plastic stud on his wristband. Jared and I both have orange ones – guest passes, Gethin says. He has a handful of them – although even with a dozen of the things, I can tell he's still reluctant to hand one over to me. I refer you to my previous statement.

Steffan peers at my wristband. "Still doesn't say VIP, though, does it?" he cackles, and then he actually does a little dance, shuffling his feet about and chanting, "VIP, VIP..."

"Loser."

"VIP."

"Seriously."

We leave them to get their act together.


The air smells of hot, dry grass trampled underfoot. It smells of diesel, of cider and cigarettes and burgers and ice cream and the ends of things. The end of the summer. The end of us: of Steffan and Jared and me.

"You want to get a drink?" Jared asks.

"Thinking about it, yeah. Just a water or something – I'm dying."

"Dying?" He raises an eyebrow at me.

"Yes. Dying. Literally." I slump sideways theatrically, dropping onto the grass. It hadn't occurred to me that the ground would be *quite* so hard...

I can feel the dry grass stems prickling against the back of my neck, against my arms. I can feel the sun on my face – even now, this late in the summer, and even with my eyes closed (playing dead, remember?) it paints a wash of reds and oranges on the inside of my eyelids. And then everything goes cold and dark. I open my eyes and look up to see Jared standing over me, blocking the light. The sun behind him gives him a halo as he stretches a hand down to help me up.

"Dying?" he says again, more pointedly this time, as he watches me brush dead grass out of my hair.

"*Actually* dying. Fell over and everything. You did see the falling over, didn't you?"

I'd hate to have to do it again.


The bar tent is the smaller (but only just) of the two main festival tents. A long wooden bar has been installed on plastic matting and a handful of staff and stewards are lugging crates of bottles from the open flap at the far end, where several vans have pulled up to unload supplies. Why they didn't just park at this end is beyond me, but there you go. Two barmen are rigging up beer taps on the bar, and another is rolling a small metal barrel along the mats.

Jared trots up to the bar and leans across. Without looking up, one of the guys working on the taps jerks a thumb back over his shoulder. Jared asks him something, but the barman shakes his head – and with a smile, Jared darts behind the bar.

There's few enough people here, and yet there's an atmosphere, an "end of summer" feeling. It's in the way the breeze is picking up. You can see it in the way the light fades fast at the end of each day – not like the evenings of July which stretch on for ever. Now, the darkness comes earlier and it comes fast. But by the time the nights close in, I won't be afraid of the dark. I won't be afraid to sleep. I won't look for my mother's face in crowds and I won't catch myself thinking that I heard her voice. Because every ending is a beginning; where one thing finishes, another thing starts, and I'm ready to let go. To move forward.

A crash from somewhere near the bar draws my attention back to the tent. A steward has dropped a box of cables in front of a small platform set up near the end of the bar. Judging by the table with laptops and leads spilling off it – not to mention the guy wearing a massive pair of headphones around his neck – it's a makeshift DJ booth. The DJ laughs and scoots around the table to help the steward pick up the wires – and I can't help but think he looks familiar. He's in flip-flops and board shorts, and his T-shirt has got some kind of record label logo on it, but my brain's telling me that's not how I've seen him dressed before. And I *do* know him. He's a few years older than us, definitely – not even still in college, by the look of him, but I *know* I know him.

"What are you scowling at?" Jared reappears and hands me a plastic bottle of water, straight out of the fridge.

"The DJ dude. Can't figure out where I know him from."

Jared takes a swig from his own bottle and looks over. "It's Will," he says, screwing the cap back onto his water – and either the DJ hears him or he realizes he's being watched, because that's the exact moment he picks to look up and over at us. He looks thoughtful, then nods at Jared in recognition.

Now I remember how I know him: that's Will Ellis.

He was way, way above us in school – like I said, he must have left college by now – but his brother Alex was pretty well known around town. "Was" being the operative word, because, a couple of years back, pothead Alex thought it would be an awesome idea to get into a car and drive while he was off his face. Two weeks after he passed his driving test. One twisty road, one car going far too fast and driven by a pot-fiend. One single-lane humpback bridge and one car coming the other way, minding its own business. While Alex walked away without a scratch, both the adults in the other car were killed instantly, the reports said; only their three-month-old baby in the back seat survived.

Everyone knows about Alex Ellis, and that's why it's such a shame that, from what I remember, his older brother Will's a really nice guy. Wherever he goes, whatever he does, he will always be "Alex Ellis's older brother"; tainted by it. Haunted by it.

Following Jared's lead, I make my way towards the DJ, stepping over thick electrical cables which have yet to be taped down and picking my way through jumbles of connectors. Will hops down from the platform and nods by way of greeting. "Jared."

I didn't think it was possible for anyone to be *less* chatty than Jared. Wrong.

They move in for one of those complicated handshakes which turns into an awkward man-hug; you know the kind of thing – one part chest-bump to one part back-slap-and-nod. It's the most relaxed I think I've ever seen Jared around anyone except Steffan, and that's saying something. I watch him as he and Will talk, their voices low. The strange light in the tent makes the creases at the corners of his eyes look deeper than they are. The last of the summer sun has darkened his freckles even further, and they're scattered like stars across the bridge of his nose. He runs his hand back through his hair as he laughs at something Will says, and I glance at the DJ. He does have lines – real ones, both around his eyes and across his forehead – and it's a surprise to see the beginnings of a streak of grey in his dark hair, close to his temple. How can that be? How can someone that I remember from school (even if they were at the opposite end of it to me) have grey hair? What does that even mean? That we're already on the downward spiral, locked in from cradle to grave?

They're both looking at me, almost like they're waiting for something.

Oh. They *are* waiting for something, aren't they? I can tell by the patient look in Will's eyes and the amused expression on Jared's face.

"Sorry. Miles away – what?"

"I said I was sorry to hear about your mum," Will repeats, for my benefit.

Of all the things to miss hearing. "Thanks," I mumble. There's not a lot else I can say, is there – and by now the response is automatic, conditioned and pre-programmed. It's What We Say To Condolences, isn't it? It's what everyone expects.

"Shitty deal," Will carries on. "Bad enough when something happens in your family. Worse when everyone thinks it's their business. Some people have a hard time coping with that." He studies me carefully, blue-grey eyes travelling across my face. "But you look like the type to be alright."

"You know the type, do you?" I ask. He's taken me by surprise.

He half-smiles, squints down at his feet and then looks straight back at me as he steps away and swings himself back onto the stage. "I know the type."

And with that, he nods goodbye and is back behind his little desk, pulling his headphones up over his ears and jabbing at buttons as he gets on with his set-up. It's how we leave him.

"How d'you know Will, then?" I ask Jared as we push our way out of the bar tent. There's now a steady stream of people making their way in, and the staff are starting to look a little panicked. The noise level is rising as more people with different coloured wristbands filter in searching for the bar. There's a little group right by the exit (or the entrance, I guess – it depends which way you look at it) who have a drink in each hand and a small pile of empties between them. As we pass, they count to three and down what looks like a full cup of cider each, like they'll find their hopes and dreams at the bottom of a plastic pint glass… Or maybe they just want to drown their fears. But the thing about fear that not many people seem to realize is it can swim.

Jared's gaze is fixed on the valley. "Court," he says, "and then visiting."

Of course. If I did the maths in my head (which I'm not going to, because, *maths*...) I'm fairly sure I'll work out that Will's brother was in court at about the same time as Jared's father – last time around, anyway. Both cases rumbled on for ever. Mind you, I'm not even going to consider the logistics of visiting a prison and how that all shakes down, because everything I know about it comes from repeats of *Prison Break* – and I'm going to go out on a limb and assume that this isn't exactly the *best* basis for comparison.

I had no idea that Jared and Will knew each other that well. I doubt Steffan does, either. It's another piece of Jared that feels like a secret, another piece of the puzzle. A puzzle I'm beginning to think he's letting me figure out – and before this trip, I would never have expected that either.

Everyone knows everyone round here...or at least they *think* they do. Because now I don't believe we ever truly know anyone. We only get to see what they show us, what they are on the outside. We get to see their masks; if we're very lucky, we get to see the scars underneath them. We see flashes, glimpses; always moving and changing like a kaleidoscope. We give different pieces of ourselves to different people – friend, parent, child, teacher – and we trust that no one ever tries to join them all up. We split

285

ourselves apart in an attempt to belong wherever we can, and then we wonder why we don't know who we are.

In the tent behind us, there's a synthesized siren followed by a distorted howl and a loud spinback...and Will's at work. He's got better taste in music than either Jared or Steffan, I'll give him that – and an appreciative cheer goes up from inside the bar. I turn and look back into the tent. They're testing the floodlights, switching them on and off and on and off, and I have to raise my hand to shield my eyes from the glare, but I can still see him. He's standing behind his laptops and his decks; a hand lifting his headphones up to one ear while the other hand's in the air in something that looks like triumph. Already there's a little knot of bodies directly in front of him, watching and listening. He looks so in control, and there was something so calm, so measured about him – about the way he spoke, the way he moved – that it gives me hope. People move forward, move on. They have to, in the end, don't they?

The main tent – the one we saw from across the valley – is much bigger on the inside than I had expected. The stage is taller, too, looming over me. There are lights rigged up on metal girders high above, and on supports which have been bolted into the ground. Someone has woven a daisy chain through the one nearest to me. It's impressive. I've always been rubbish at stuff like that – you need good nails to punch through the stem without tearing it, and I chew my nails, so. Although, to be fair, I *have* been doing better. Well, had. Sort of fell off the nail-chewing wagon a few weeks ago, didn't I? Never mind.

The tent must have gone up earlier in the summer: the grass inside, only partly covered by rubber matting, is green and damp. I can't quite stop myself from bending down to touch it, to rub it between my fingers. It's cool and soft and not at all like the grass outside. It seems strange that the two can feel so different – even smell so different – just for the sake of a little shade.

At the far side of the tent from the stage, beside a bank of seating, there's another much smaller platform. And on it there's a row of cameras.

Oh, Steffan's just going to be *thoroughly* obnoxious now, isn't he?

# twenty-six

Steffan is pacing. Up and down, up and down, up and down, wearing a rut in the ground that's almost as deep as the one made by the tractor. He's flexing his fingers, wiggling them, keeping them constantly in motion in time with the music from the stage. And he's gone a sort of beige.

Steffan is nervous.

I'm not surprised; if I were him, I'd be terrified.

Since we got here, the place has filled up. And I mean *filled*. There are now people everywhere. The bar tent is heaving and the stage tent is a clammy, humid mass of bodies. It's sticky. And pungent.

The violin case is sitting on the ground. Steffan's still pacing up and down by the side entrance to the tent – or what I guess you'd call the stage door. He looks like he's going to throw up.

I've never seen him this nervous. Gradually, all the

bravado has fallen away until what we're left with is the real Steffan. Not the rugby player, not the guy with the crappy old car who drives too fast and swears like a trooper and pretends to be untouchable... but the Steffan underneath it all.

Because Steffan's just like the rest of us; he wears a mask too. It's one of the things that keeps us together, this strange little alliance. We see each other's masks; see the strings holding them on – and more than that, now we can see through them. And when the mask slips in public, we cover the gaps, run interference. We always will.

The real Steffan is quieter than he lets on. He worries more. He hurts more. He *cares* more. That's what he hides behind his mask.

Watching him pacing, I feel nervous *for* him. I can't tell if it's my heart or the bass drum onstage making the inside of my ribs rattle. I can taste Steffan's fear in my mouth, as sharp as if it's mine; of course I can. It's what we do, for better or worse. He's pacing and he's flexing his fingers and then – suddenly – he stops. His eyes close, just for a second, and when he opens them he's transformed.

He picks up the case and he looks right through us – both of us, waiting with him. And without a word, he pushes his way into the tent.

"Come on," says Jared. "Don't want to miss his big moment, do we?"

* * *

The tent is absolutely rammed; after all, we're into the big-hitting slots now. I pray to every god I can think of – and a few I've probably just made up – that Gethin's band have improved since the last time I heard them play. If not for Gethin's sake (or his dad's, having presumably paid for this) then for Steffan's.

The band who were on before them are taking a bow and filing off the stage with their instruments. Who'd have thought you could get *that* many trumpets on one stage? The audience swells and shifts, the people who'd been watching at the front falling back while others move up to take their place. Some guy staggers as he passes me, waving a plastic pint glass overhead. I only manage to avoid the beer-shower that follows by jumping back and landing on somebody else's toes. "Sorry!" They either don't hear me or don't care. Probably both.

Gethin knocks over his mic stand. There's a good start; feedback howls around the tent and everyone groans.

If I stand on tiptoes, I can just see Steffan behind him at the back of the stage, holding his violin. The lights flit across his face and then spin away. He looks calm.

He looks like he belongs.

He does. He belongs up there with the lights and the crowd and the music – not stuck in a small town where no

290

one will ever hear him or see him except for the gossips, who'll tear your skin off in strips until you're nothing more than one giant exposed nerve. He *belongs* up there, and I finally understand that it's not just my mother I have to let go. I have to let him go too.

To give them their credit, they've got better. A lot better. They're somewhere on the borderline between "tolerable" and "alright" now. In fact, they may even be inching into "good", but let's not be too hasty.

And Gethin's still a dick, so there's that.

I find myself swaying slightly to the music. All around me, people are dancing. They're laughing and they're drinking beer that's a little too warm or a little too flat – and they don't care. The tent smells of beer and sweat and damp and people…and life. It's alive.

The drumbeats vibrate through the ground like a heartbeat, through me. They pulse against my ribs – and they're even in time.

And there, suddenly, is Steffan.

The lights find him and he lifts his bow. He moves across the stage like he was born to it; side to side, his eyes open but not seeing. There but not there. The band around him nod their heads to the rhythm, and somebody, somewhere, starts to clap. Slowly, steadily, in time. I didn't even notice when the drums stopped, when all the other instruments died away and left nothing but Steffan playing alone.

The notes wrap around me, over me. They fill the air and everyone in the tent is clapping along…and just like that, the rest of the band burst back in and there's music everywhere and Steffan's still playing, faster and faster, and I can see the smile on his face from here as he stamps one foot and he plays and he moves and he plays.

And from somewhere behind me, a hand takes mine. I know the feel of it already: rougher than you'd think, warm in the heat of the tent.

He pulls me back towards him as I turn to face him, drawing me in. His eyes search my face, his other hand brushing my hair away and tucking it behind my ear. He looks so serious, so completely centred on me, that I could almost believe there was nothing else in the world. That there was no one else.

He lifts his hand, lifts mine, lifts *our hands*, the fingers entwined, and he looks at me. Really looks at me.

And then the corners of his eyes crease and his mouth twitches and his lips part into a smile…and he spins me away and around, and we're dancing and I can't tell if it's the world that's spinning or if it's me. All I know is that I don't want it to stop.

If I could stop time, just once, this would be it. This moment; this *now*. This would be it – here in this tent with

Steffan playing and the crowd hearing him and Jared spinning me around and around, pulling me close and then twirling me away; his eyes watching me. His smile all mine.

This is the memory I want to save. This one.

I can let go of everything else.


I don't even know when the music stopped; I didn't hear it. All I can hear is the ringing in my ears and the sound of applause. And Jared's pulling me into him again. I can feel his hand on my waist, on the small of my back; his fingers wrapped around mine. Close up, he smells of heat and of dry, dusty grass. Of smoke. Of warmth.


He smells of beginnings. Beginnings set in motion a long time ago and overlooked. Beginnings which no number of endings could bury.

I rest the side of my head against his shoulder, breathing him in.

His hand moves from my back to my hair, smoothing it. His fingers trace the line of my neck, grazing my jaw. His thumb brushes my collarbone.

And the light is blinding as the path opens up in front of me.

* * *

We started this with a funeral. It ends with a wake. Our wake: Steffan, Jared and Limpet's. The paradox that somehow worked. This is how we bow out. This is where we end. When we look back – and we will, sometime – this will be the moment we see. This is the ending and the beginning. This is all of it. All the mess and all the masks forgotten. All our scars charted and mapped. This is what it always was; what it was always going to be.

When Steffan comes to find us, his eyes shining and a drink already in his hand, he sees Jared's arm around my waist and he winks and he raises his glass to us as we elbow towards him and throw our arms around his shoulders, because he already knew.

Of course he knew. He'd known all along...

You know what a limpet is, really? It's a shellfish which attaches itself to something and holds on for dear life. It holds on so tightly that it's impossible to remove without actually *killing* the stubborn little bastard. A limpet would rather see itself destroyed than let go of whatever it is that it loves.

Sometimes we have to let go.

We cling to the ships that carried us, even as they founder. We hold fast to them as they sink, not caring that they will drag us down with them into the cold and the dark.

We follow the wrong stars, keeping our course even as the quicksand closes over our heads.

We hide behind our masks, too afraid to let anyone see what's on the inside. We worry the scars are all that anyone will see: the bruises, the cuts. The damage we've sustained. We're frightened that the damage is all we are; that it will define us always and for ever. We're scared that the cuts will make us sharper, that we will cut in our turn.

Our damage, our history – it doesn't define us. *We* define *it*.

No more Limpet. She can go. I don't need her any more.

No more pretending, no more hiding.

It's time to move on.

Picture me dancing, somewhere on the top of a hill where the grass is sunburned brown and there's music and laughter and the air smells of spilled beer and hay; the ends of things and the beginnings of others.

Picture me with my hair streaming behind me, laughing as confetti dances in the wind.

Picture me as these things, because that's how I'll be. *That* is who I am.

And my name; my real name…?

My name's Rosie.

What's yours?

# acknowledgements

*The Last Summer of Us* will always be a story close to my heart. To be able to send Limpet, Jared and Steffan out into the world is a huge privilege and I owe an immense debt to everyone involved for their support.

To everyone at Usborne who has worked so hard to turn what started as just words into a beautiful book: thank you. Special thanks, too, go to Rebecca Hill, Becky Walker, Sarah Stewart and Anne Finnis – I can't quite find the words (ironically enough) to describe how grateful I am, and how welcome you have all made me feel. Anna Howorth and Amy Dobson: thank you for being brilliant, for putting up with my daft questions, and for not batting an eyelid when I sent you an envelope full of rocks!

To my agent Juliet Mushens, who immediately understood the story I wanted to tell and who wouldn't let me stop until I'd told it. Thank you for never letting me back down – and thank you to Sarah Manning at The Agency Group for keeping the wheels turning.

To my friends Kim and Will: Kim, who read an early draft and whose enthusiasm gave me a raft to cling to. Will, for always being one of the Good Ones.

To the fabulous ladies of Bath: Caroline and Dionne; Lisa, Debbie, Nic and Lou – I owe you all.

And to my family, without whose unwavering support I would be lost. You are my map, my lantern and my home.

# *about the author*

Like Limpet, Steffan and Jared, Maggie Harcourt was born and raised in Wales, where she grew up dreaming of summer road trips and telling stories for a living. As well as studying medieval literature at UCL, Maggie has variously worked as a PA, a hotel chambermaid and for a French chef before realizing her dreams and beginning to write full time.

Maggie now lives just outside Bath, and still visits Wales to wander the Carmarthenshire beaches and countryside.

 maggiehaha.tumblr.com

 maggieharcourt

 @maggieharcourt

# Q&A with Maggie

*What was your inspiration for writing* The Last Summer of Us*?*
I think I'd been carrying Limpet around in my head for a long
time. I grew up in west Wales, in a fairly small town where there
wasn't a lot to do when I was fifteen. I was visiting a place called
Henllan, and I had an idea for a story about a group of friends on
a road trip around places very like that one. I even went as far as
writing something and typing it out on a typewriter I'd saved up
for. It didn't get very far, but I never forgot Limpet – and when I
was back in the area, I picked up the story again…and here we
are. In fact, the river at Henllan ended up being a direct
inspiration for the place where Limpet, Jared and Steffan meet
after the funeral.

I wanted the story to be very specifically set in Wales and
rooted in areas like Carmarthenshire and Ceredigion and
Pembrokeshire: I am Welsh, after all, and I had never really been
able to find books about the places and characters I could see my

friends in when I was growing up. More than anything, though, I wanted to talk about things like love and loss and friendship and hope, because we all go through them. We all feel them and the way we handle them helps make us who we are.

*The novel explores grief and how it changes a family; what message were you intending to pass on to your reader?*
Grief does change people, sometimes in big ways and sometimes in small ones. There are different kinds of grief, too: grief for a person or a relationship or a place (and there's even *hiraeth*, the infuriatingly untranslatable Welsh word for a kind of nostalgic longing for the place you come from. More than just homesickness, it's a sense of grief for what has been, and what could have been.) but it doesn't have to change us for the bad and it doesn't have to take away who we were before. We don't have to let it.

*What was it like writing a character who is experiencing such emotional turmoil?*
Limpet had to be written as honestly as possible, and sometimes that was hard. Not just because she needed to be someone you feel you know, but because she represents something that people really go through. We all lose people, in one way or another – so to hold back felt like it would be a massive disservice both to readers and to her.

I tried to be as emotionally open as I could – my own mother died a few years ago, and while I wasn't in the same position as

Limpet, I felt that having gone through that grieving process meant I could understand her better and make her more real.

At the same time, it would have been a pretty bleak experience all round if it was all death, all grief, all the time – because that's not true either, is it? Trying to show that Limpet was more than that; that grief wasn't all she was and that it hadn't taken away who she was deep down, mattered just as much. Finding a balance between the two – both for her and for me – could be a bit of a challenge, and I definitely had a few days where I just wanted to sit under the table with a blanket over my head and pretend I wasn't there! But when it felt like I'd got her right, it was worth it.

*If you could tell your teen self anything, what would it be?*
I left home and went to university in London at seventeen, so I could easily fill a big, big book with advice I could have done with knowing then. Things like: "That haircut? No." Or: "Stop refusing to change lines on the Tube. Seriously. It shouldn't take you a YEAR to get past this. That's ridiculous."

But if there was only one thing, it would be this: live. There'll be things you're glad you did, and things you wish you hadn't… and both of those are okay, because you shouldn't let anything stop you from living (not even a different Tube line). Life is a gift: why would you want to give it back unopened?

# Coming soon from Maggie Harcourt

Flora "doesn't do people", not since the Incident that led to her leaving school midway through her GCSEs. The Incident that led to her being diagnosed with bipolar II. The Incident that left her in pieces.

Until Hal arrives. He's researching a story about a missing World War I soldier, and he wants Flora's help. Flora used to love history before the Incident, but spending so much time with Hal is her worst nightmare. Yet as they begin to piece together the life of the missing soldier – a life of lost love, secrets and lies – Flora finds a piece of herself falling for Hal...

## Out in Spring 2020

# Also by Maggie Harcourt

EVERYONE'S A FAN OF SOMEONE

UNCONVENTIONAL

"A gorgeous one-of-a-kind novel, perfect for fans of Rainbow Rowell"
*Maximum Pop!*

Maggie Harcourt

Six conventions. A girl with a clipboard.
A boy with two names — and one night that
changes everything...